MATTHIAS POLITYCKI

*TRANSLATED FROM THE GERMAN
BY ANTHEA BELL*

Peirene

Jenseits–
novelle

AUTHOR

Matthias Politycki, born in 1955, has published over 20 novels and poetry collections. He is ranked among the most successful literary authors writing in German. His books have sold over 200,000 copies and have been translated into several languages, including French and Italian. *Next World Novella* was first published in German in 2009.

TRANSLATOR

Anthea Bell is one of the most renowned British translators. She has rendered numerous literary works from German and French into English. She is, however, best known for her translations of the French *Asterix* comics. Anthea Bell received her OBE for services to literature and literary translation in 2010.

MEIKE ZIERVOGEL
PEIRENE PRESS

This novella deals with the weighty subjects of marriage and death in an impressively light manner. Shifting realities evolve with a beautiful sense of irony and wit. It is a tone that allows us to reflect, without judgment, on misunderstandings, contradictory perceptions and the transience of life.

First published in Great Britain in 2011 by
Peirene Press Ltd
17 Cheverton Road
London N19 3BB
www.peirenepress.com

Reprinted 2012

Originally published in German as
JENSEITSNOVELLE
Copyright © 2009 by Hoffmann und Campe Verlag, Hamburg

This translation © Anthea Bell, 2011

This work has been translated with the financial support of the
Goethe-Institut through German Foreign Office funding.

Sponsored by Deutscher Literaturfonds.

ISBN 978-0-9562840-3-7

Designed by Sacha Davison Lunt
Photographic image: PIER / Stone / Getty Images
Printed and bound by T J International, Padstow, Cornwall

MATTHIAS POLITYCKI

TRANSLATED FROM THE GERMAN
BY ANTHEA BELL

Peirene

Next
World
Novella

If only it hadn't been for that smell! As if Doro had forgotten to change the water for the flowers, as if their stems had begun to rot overnight, filling the air with the sweet-sour aroma of decay. Schepp noticed it at once, that subtle sense of something Other in the midst of ordinary life, slightly skewing the morning. From the far end of his room autumn sunlight came flooding in, bathing everything in a golden or russet glow – the *chaise-longue* in the corner was a patch of melting colour. They'd have to open a window to let all that light out later. Schepp stood there, blinking at his world gently flowing around him, a world of stucco moulding and decorative wallpaper, book-lined walls, chairs with silk covers. Checking the way his hair lay over his bald patch, stroking the back of his head, he told himself that he was a happy man.

Not least because of Doro, whose own hair, pinned up, mingled black and silver, he could see above the back of the desk chair. At one side he glimpsed the kimono she liked to wear when she sat in that chair, editing what he had written the day before. Since the children had left home, she had wanted to resume her career. That had pleased him. Not only did he go to bed late, he also got up late, so if Doro had fallen asleep over her editing, wedged at an awkward angle between the desk and the chair as she was today, he would just shake his head, because he couldn't have put into words all that he felt.

Oddly enough, as regularly as he had found her here before, he had written almost nothing since his operation, so was there anything to be edited? I'm still dreaming, he told himself as he moved quietly across the fishbone-patterned parquet towards the sun and the desk and the big vase standing on the floor with the decaying gladioli in it, and Doro.

Before he planted a kiss on her neck, stealing up quietly like a man newly in love, a few of the little wooden segments of the parquet creaking slightly, a fly buzzing somewhere (but even that sounded familiar and homely), before he bent over Doro, to the little mole at the base of her throat that he knew so well – any minute now she would wake with a start and look askance at him, half indignant, half affectionate – he suddenly registered a stack of paper on the desk, her reading glasses, a packet of aspirins, a water glass that had been knocked over and a dark mark on the leather inlay of the desktop, with her fountain pen beside it. Once again she had forgotten to put the cap back on it. He was about to pick it up when he remembered, and no, he wasn't dreaming any more, remembered yesterday evening and the new waitress who had given him such a long, intent smile as he was leaving the bar. Schepp was standing directly behind the chair where Doro sat so still, only the wing of the chair-back kept her from tipping over, and he smiled at this thought for a few seconds. Well, Hinrich, he said to himself, grinning at the place where he thought he detected a last reflection of the night before, you may be sixty-five but the ladies still have time for you. Then he bent over Doro. Once again the smell hit him, an entirely strange smell now, a sweetish aroma mingled with the odour of sweat and urine and – he shrank back, his mouth gaping.

Gulped, gasped.

How he made his way around the desk he didn't know. He clung to it with both hands, hardly daring to look up. Doro? She sat there before him, her features relaxed, entirely at peace, her skin grey. The left-hand corner of her mouth drooped, a thread of saliva hanging from it. It had dried where it ended on her chin. Her lips were slightly open, her tongue lolled awkwardly in her mouth, looking swollen. But worst of all were her eyes, almost but not entirely closed, so that you could see the whites and a bit of the irises, as if she had pulled her lower lids down at the last moment.

I don't understand, thought Schepp, understanding.

It's not true, Schepp decided.

Everything will be all right again, Schepp assured himself, and at the same time he was overcome by the certainty that he was choking.

'At least say something,' he whispered finally. 'Just one word.'

He wanted so much to take Doro in his arms, to hug her until she was gasping for breath and stopped playing this game. But there was nothing he could do, he saw that, he felt it, he knew it. He couldn't even pluck up the courage to whimper; he remained immobilized, breathing as shallowly as possible.

At least it hadn't been rotting flower stems that he had smelt when he had come into the room, he knew that now. Leaning on the desk, Schepp looked into what could still be seen of Doro's eyes. He dared not close them. How long, he wondered, had she been sitting here dead, waiting for him? He attempted to take her pulse; he had to try several times; he feared the chill of her wrist so much that he flinched as soon as he touched it; he was sure, in any case, that there was nothing to be felt. Should he call a doctor? Oughtn't he call a doctor?

He stared across the parquet and into the great void; he saw himself immobilized at his mother's deathbed because he could not bring himself to touch her in farewell, he saw himself finally, wordlessly, placing his hand on her forehead – and that immediately brought him back to the hard, oaken presence of the desk on which one of his manuscripts appeared to be lying. Obviously Doro had been editing it and, in her usual way, annotating the pages, summarizing her impressions; the top sheet was three-quarters covered with her firm handwriting. Or rather, only the first lines were written in that familiar script, then the characters visibly slipped sideways. Schepp bent closer to the page; the letters appeared very untidy, Doro would never have set them down like that, not in full possession of her senses. Soon whole words were sliding away from her; here and there the paper had absorbed water from the glass she had knocked over, and the ink had run. Schepp almost reached towards the manuscript to put it somewhere dry. Only then to embrace Doro, warm her, perhaps put her to bed and sit beside her until she awoke. But the sight of her kept him at a distance, the sight of her face frozen into a mask, alarmingly peaceful, already alarmingly unfamiliar, smooth, almost unwrinkled, surprisingly like the face of her sister, who was still under fifty, how strange. To think, reflected Schepp, trying to hide in the shelter of his hands, to think that you grow younger in death. Then his throat tightened as a great wave of misery washed over him. When he could move again, the clock on the Church of the Good Shepherd was striking eleven. He hesitantly touched Doro's right hand and once more shrank from the cold skin and its waxen feel, like a layer of varnish. Finally he took her left arm, which had slipped off the desk, holding it by the sleeve of her kimono and carefully replacing it where he thought it belonged, beside the manuscript. Her hand was swollen and purplish-red, her forearm a shade of violet. Schepp stared at the pale pressure marks that, despite his caution, he had left on Doro's arm. The longer he looked, the more blood seemed to flow back into it. The silence of the room closed gently around her again. Overwhelmed, Schepp breathed in the smell of death.

Finally he looked back at the stack of paper that Doro had left for him. Yes – it hit him like a sudden revelation – that was the first, the most important thing to do. He had to read those pages, find out what her last message was. How relieved he felt all at once! As if some kind of hope could be derived from that act. The idea that another action might be more appropriate, considering that he had spent half his life with the deceased, did not cross his mind.

At first it seemed as if his shaking hands were holding a long, unusually long set of editorial comments. Beneath the top sheet, where the handwritten lines soon became crooked and agitated until finally all the words were in the middle of the page, lay many other sheets, meticulously filled with Doro's familiar handwriting. Under those was a typewritten manuscript, the first page at the bottom of the stack and untitled; only after leafing forwards and back for a while did he realize that this was a fragment he had discarded long since and far from being a serious work of scholarship. How had Doro found it, even thought it worth editing – and she had obviously been editing it for days – this old, forgotten text of his? He hadn't concealed or destroyed it, he had just forgotten when he last had had it in his hands. The longer he thought about it, the more certain he felt that Doro had been looking for something, something else. Schepp fell into all kinds of speculations; he hardly noticed the sheets of paper slipping from his hands and falling on the patterned wood of the parquet. The throbbing in his throat grew worse and worse, and a rushing in his ears began to make him dizzy.

Once he had opened the window he felt better. He tried not to shrink from the chilly presence of Doro waiting for him on the other side of the desk, with a smell about her that would certainly have embarrassed her very much when she was alive. When you're dead, she had once whispered in his ear before going to sleep, you can't smell anyone any more, isn't that sad? Schepp felt ashamed on her behalf, and whispered that there was no need for her to feel ashamed, he loved her all the same; perhaps he loved her even more for her inviolability and the stillness she radiated, had radiated even in life, had he ever told her that?

He replaced the cap on her fountain pen, righted the empty glass, retrieved the scattered sheets of paper from the floor and hesitated again, staring at the last page of Doro's comments. They read:

… turned into its opposite, the gentle wind above, the rejoicing lake beneath. 'It is good to cross the great water.' But without you, Schepp, do you understand, without you. As far as I'm concerned, and now I will say it once and for all, you can go straight to Hell! Along with Hanni and Nanni and Lina and Tina and
    whatever they might be called. Your
    I'm sorry, my head
    suddenly hurts again,
    like when I

Had Doro really written that? The spaces between the words became larger and larger, the rest was illegible, or no, at the bottom of the page, on the right-hand side, there was a little more in a shaky, entirely unfamiliar hand. It took Schepp some time to decipher it.

and now this too
well we'll
talk about it

Doro's last words – how they blurred before his
eyes! The pattern of the parquet – how it stretched
away to the surrounding bookcases, which held his
publications and special editions as well as standard
works and volumes of commentaries, and on which
were arranged all the things he had brought back
from lecture tours and guest professorships, together
with photographs of the children, Pia radiant just
before her wedding, Louisa looking sulky because
he never had time in the evening for anyone but
his 'silly old Chinese people' – it was all there, but
now so far removed that he saw none of it. Schepp
had been left desperately alone. All he had were the
sheets of paper that Doro had written for him.

But written in what kind of confusion, and by
which Doro? Obviously she hadn't been entirely in
her right mind; he'd never known her to sound so
out of control, so wild, so forceful. What on earth
had come over her? Doro, that fragile little woman
whose discretion he had always admired! He wanted
to start reading at once, from the beginning – 'As
far as I'm concerned' – no, something wrong there
– 'As far as I'm concerned, you can go straight to
Hell', and when had she ever addressed him by his
surname? Was she making fun of him?

It was no good, he *had* to read it. Yes, maybe he ought to have let the children know first, but did a few more minutes make any difference? Yes, he ought to have called a doctor to fill out a death certificate. But which doctor should he have called, when Doro wasn't even registered with a GP? And then it really would have been over, they'd take what was left of her away, and emptiness would move in, first into her favourite places, soon even into the most remote nooks and crannies – no! There was time enough for that in what life he had left. Gesticulating at the room, right index and little fingers extended as if in full flow, talking himself into true lecturer's mode, Schepp strode back and forth, punching accentuated reprimands into the air with his fist, until he came to a halt by the window. And saw that life outside was still going on as usual.

He would just stand there, then, stand there until he finally fell over, or woke up, or until the world came to an end. Standing like that also meant that he didn't have to look at Doro. What had she died of, anyway, when she had never been really sick? As if her doubts about conventional medicine had kept her healthy. Apart from two or three migraines a year, she had managed very well indeed without all the check-ups and aftercare that kept her sister happy. 'No tumour, no heart problems,' she had been told after a CT scan following one of her migraines. 'Everything's in good working order.' These days people didn't just drop dead at the age of fifty-six!

Although she herself used to be preoccupied with that very thing. It was how he had met her in the first place, he was then a mere Teaching Fellow whilst she was already a Lecturer in the Faculty. Out of the blue, she had told him about her fear, her great fear of the cold, dark lake whose shores you'd reach immediately after you died, only to die there a second time. Or whatever it could be called when you were already dead. He had almost let slip a stupid remark, saw the tears in her eyes just in time.

So now it's happened, thought Schepp, now she really has gone to the place she's dreaded all her life. And what about me? I promised to hold her hand there, and I've failed her. Had she already reached the lake? Was she standing on the shore scanning the water for an island, the island that, during their life together, he had hoped she would find there? Perhaps she had already taken her first steps into the water, bravely, without any fuss, in her usual way. Perhaps she was swimming with calm and steady strokes towards a second death? No, no, Schepp was sure that whatever Doro was doing on the other side, at least she wasn't doing *that*; she had always promised not to.

It had been in the winter term of 1979–80. He had been adoring her from afar for two years, ever since she had suddenly moved into the room opposite his. Whenever he had brought over a pot of green tea for her, she had been intently studying the I Ching. He was in his mid-thirties, just completing the thesis on ancient Chinese script that would qualify him as a lecturer, and well on the way to becoming number one in Germany in his field, because there *was* no number two working on the same subject. Nine years younger, she didn't have her PhD yet, but already had a full-time appointment. She was the constant subject of gossip at the Institute, perhaps even throughout the entire Berlin's Free University. Dorothee Wilhelmine Renate, Countess von Hagelstein, who apparently had been two years ahead of her age group at school, and who had spent a year in Taiwan before beginning her university studies; Dorothee Wilhelmine Renate, Countess von Hagelstein, whose forebears had made their fortune importing Chinese art, also acquiring a rather dubious reputation under the Third Reich; Dorothee Wilhelmine Renate, Countess von Hagelstein, courted by everyone in Faculty II, Sinology, including the professor, who had created the post of assistant for her with no trouble at all, and who then also saw to her seminars on 'The History and Theory of Feng Shui', and on 'Women's Poetry during the Tang Dynasty', and of course, also, every term, on the subject of her dissertation: 'Three Thousand Years of the Wisdom and Prophecies of the I Ching'; 'The Flowing Together of All Things in the I Ching'; 'The Dark Lines of the I Ching'.

When Schepp crossed the corridor in silence to place the pot of tea beside her on the desk, she was usually hunched over the commentaries of the emperors and philosophers of ancient China, surrounded by the sixty-four signs of the old oracular book. She had hung them on the walls of her room in an order that placed the water signs at the centre – yes, even a scholar strictly interested in philology, like Schepp, knew his way around the I Ching, not so much because it was regarded as sacred by soothsayers, and probably by Countess von Hagelstein too, as because the entire intellectual life of ancient China had been concerned with its interpretation. It was a subject to which grave and serious statesmen and scholars had turned their minds, even Confucius – Kung Tze – whom Schepp venerated. He suspected that the little countess, who in spite of her youth seemed entirely absorbed in research and scholarship, interpreted it in mystical terms. Sometimes she emerged briefly from her reveries with a start when he came in. But usually she didn't even notice when he stood beside her for a few too many seconds, gazing at her wide-eyed. What could she have seen behind the thick lenses of his glasses anyway, except his pupils, a couple of sparkling pinheads? With his extremely poor eyesight, Schepp was lucky to get out of the room again without bumping into everything. No, he was certain that nothing could bind this perfect young woman to a man like him. Even his school-leaving exams had been a test that he had passed successfully only because his teachers recognized his talent, and his studies had been financed by a foundation for gifted students. It was his place to be grateful and not ask for more than his due.

But one day in the late autumn of 1979, when he was still addressing Doro as Fräulein Dorothee although she had specially asked him to drop the 'Fräulein', she had looked up as soon as he had placed the teapot on to her desk, and, even more surprisingly, had asked if he had any idea what the next world would be like. After all, in the Faculty he was considered a specialist on Kung Tze; she, on the other hand, felt a greater sympathy with Taoism. So ... In fact here Schepp agreed with Confucius, who held that it was not worthwhile dwelling on what we could not know. But of course, he said as forcefully he could, he had an idea about the next world, in fact an extremely precise idea. There wasn't one. He didn't want to live for ever in any case, he added defiantly; there was an end to everything, even a sausage had *two* ends. The next moment, he would have been prepared to convert to Tibetan Red Hat Buddhism, but Fräulein Dorothee merely regarded him with her dark eyes, and the conversation was over.

Curiously enough, however, she picked up on it the next day exactly where she had broken it off. As soon as Schepp appeared in her doorway she asked him, sounding quite anxious, almost imploring, how, as a thinking human, he could say such a thing. All the cool, objective distance that constituted not a little of her magic was gone; she pleaded with him as if he were a friend who must be saved from some terrible error. There had to be something after death, she said; surely life with all its beauty couldn't end just like that? There were tears in her eyes. Then, as soon as Schepp had agreed with her, nodding vigorously, they grew even darker, and she said softly, as if he wasn't there, as if she was completely alone, that of course it wouldn't go on in as beautiful a way as before, far from it. In the Southern Commentaries on the I Ching, she came across passages in which the sign for 'lake' was curiously ambivalent, as if – unlike, for instance, the signs for 'wind', 'mountain' or 'sky' – it wasn't just referring to something joyful, which was what the Commentaries usually stressed, but also to its opposite, something dark that had to be overcome. However, none of the commentaries told you how to do that, as if the lake – ah, well, she didn't suppose the mystical side of it would interest a linguist.

Far from it. Schepp dispelled that illusion immediately. And so it was that while for two years he had known nothing about his new colleague in the Faculty apart from the rumours circulating about her, he now discovered her most secret fears in the course of a single afternoon.

After death, she said, if she understood the Southern Commentaries correctly, the process of dying only really begins when the soul is judged and purified. Sooner or later you come to a lake, its waters motionless, in the midst of a bleak landscape. From a distance it may seem like a mountain lake, only larger, much larger, and the far shore can only be vaguely discerned in the diffuse light. Indeed, all the light in that place is muted, she said; there are no colours, no smells, not a breath of wind, not a sound, and that is sufficiently terrible, but worst of all you are entirely alone, yet you must enter the cold water and swim across. Swim to the far shore where perhaps life goes on somehow or other, but that makes no real difference, for you have no chance at all of reaching the shore; your powers are bound to fail by the time you get to the middle of the lake at the latest, everyone's powers fail. Then you let yourself drift for a while, becoming colder and colder, and at last you are drawn down into the depths as if by a giant hand, and ...

And?

No 'and'. Then you are really dead, and it's all over.

For ever?

For ever. And the lake, she said, was so dark and cold, and it frightened her.

But who says, asked Schepp, that you have to go into the water? You could just stay on the shore. Or walk around the lake if you really wanted to reach the other side.

Oh, said Fräulein Dorothee, and there were tears in her eyes again, the lake exerts a magical attraction, and although you know you're sure to meet your end in it, it shimmers promisingly like a new beginning, and you can't escape it.

Schepp briefly thought of responding with a knowing grin in anticipation of a smile in return – for there was no way she could mean all this seriously – but instead ironic objections spilled out of him. Surely, he said, the lake must be full by now, full to the brim, and in fact if all the people who had died over thousands and millions of years had drowned in it, Doro probably wouldn't have to swim when her turn came, she could walk across the water dry-shod. The next moment he could have bitten his tongue off, but Fräulein Dorothee just regarded him briefly, and once again the conversation was over.

After that not a day went by when Schepp didn't think of the lake and its inhospitable shores, and the way Dorothee Wilhelmine Renate, Countess von Hagelstein shuddered at the thought of having to undress there. Sometimes he pondered whether she might enter the water fully dressed, or whether he might swim from the far side of the lake to meet her. He didn't make much progress with her that way at all. But he made headway with the cold, dark lake. By winter's end he had a very clear picture of it, could even imagine the surrounding landscape, the vague shape of a mountain pine, a wan sky flashing with distant lightning. So he was greatly surprised when Fräulein Dorothee, still in her coat, came into his room. Since that last conversation she hadn't deigned to glance at him when he had brought her pots of tea in silent plea for forgiveness. Her hair was a bit tousled; a film of perspiration gleamed on her forehead and upper lip.

Could she show him something, she asked. She knew he didn't believe in it, but now, now she could prove it. Prove that it existed. The lake. Scarcely an hour later they entered the great glass cube of Berlin's New National Gallery, which was flooded with light. The little that Schepp had found out from Fräulein Dorothee on the way amounted to the fact that on a recent visit she had discovered a picture that, she could have sworn, hadn't been hanging there before, a picture that, as far as she knew, had been missing since the war. It had suddenly turned up again without any fanfare although its reappearance should have caused a sensation. She had been deeply moved when she had suddenly been confronted with it; the original had a power at which copies merely hinted, a shattering finality in fact. It was proof.

With great determination she led him to the basement of the building – grey, carpeted floor, functional atmosphere – where suddenly her mood became reverential. She stopped in front of a gilt-framed painting perhaps one and a half metres wide by just under one metre high. In the picture ... the surprised Schepp turned to his companion, but she was gazing in silent fascination, so he had himself to come to terms with the fact that the painting showed not a cold, dark lake but a huge island, a monumental, towering wall of rock, a rocky curve around a group of cypress trees with a flickering violet-tinged sky in the background. Before the island, as Schepp's eyes became accustomed to the gloomy hues, he saw a boat making for its shore, with a white, muffled figure standing in front of a coffin draped with white cloth. He could also make out various steps and openings in the rock resembling archaic portals. Just to make sure, he glanced at the picture's title. He had already realized that a few strokes of the oars would bring a new corpse to the island, to be placed on a plinth or in one of the burial chambers. Yes, the island impressed him; there was something so fundamentally desolate about it that he imagined the peace of the dead reigning in that place as a dignified form of despair. What fate as dark as those cypresses awaited the newly dead?

Only then did Schepp focus on what little the painting showed of the cold lake itself – water so calm that it reflected the vertical walls of rock without any tremor on its surface, motionless all the way to the horizon, which was nothing but a straight line. An endless, dead sea.

How, he finally whispered to Fräulein Dorothee, did she know it was a lake? She seemed unwilling to abandon her mood of rapt attention.

Anyone could see that, she said.

He gave up on the muted whispers appropriate for a museum. Lake or not, it certainly wasn't empty; there was even an island in it, a place where life went on, as it were, for the dead. Wasn't that prospect worth something?

'Please forgive me,' Fräulein Dorothee interrupted him without taking her eyes off the picture, 'but it's not an island.'

They stood in front of the painting for a long time, so long that one of the attendants wandered over and confided in a friendly tone that this was his own favourite picture. After he had turned away to keep an eye on the other visitors lingering only briefly in front of various pictures, Fräulein Dorothee explained.

Anyone could see, she said, that the painting was intended to be surreal; it skilfully kept its real subject hidden; the island was nothing but a reflection, an illusion that the painter had added as a kind of consolation. The boat, the ferryman, the muffled figure were all concessions to the taste of the time. The whole thing might just be reflected light from the depths of the lake, designed to lure us into the next world. 'Oh, Hinrich,' she said, the words wrenched out of her, 'I don't want to go there.'

At that moment it happened: *it* because Schepp himself was not quite sure what he was doing when he began to speak, telling her that he wasn't afraid of death; he would simply die before she did and scout out the terrain for her.

'Would you really do that for me?' asked Fräulein Dorothee after a while.

Schepp nodded mutely; he could not even begin to feel certain of the full import of her question. Then he added: if he died first he'd wait for her – again, it was not like Schepp, growing bolder, to reach for Fräulein Dorothee's little clenched fist, pressing it clumsily. And then, he said, he'd take her hand and go with her, they would reach the far shore together. Or at least the island. If the island turned out to be real.

The next moment he was wishing the ground could have swallowed him up. Fräulein Dorothee took a deep, audible breath, but she was looking at him, and not even in surprise, or with amusement or indignation –

'Or we'll drown together,' she said, exhaling, also audibly. 'At least that's better than drowning alone.'

Still she did not withdraw her hand. As he turned to her slowly, looking cautiously at her through the thick lenses of his glasses, she seemed to be a hallucination which might dissolve into thin air if he regarded her too closely, translucent, untouchable, a creature from another star. And yet, and yet, she left her hand in his for an extraordinary length of time. She stood beside him, smiled at him, as if a burden had been lifted from her mind.

That decided things. In the same year, Dorothee Wilhelmine Renate, Countess von Hagelstein became Doro Schepp, rejecting a double surname, and instead of fulfilling the hopes of the East Asia department of the Faculty she soon became a mother, abandoning her dissertation and, to the horror of the entire teaching body, the promise of her glittering career. Nothing much became of the now fully qualified Dr Hinrich Schepp either, number one in the field of ancient Chinese language. His professor was able to prevent at least that.

Schepp found that he was now sitting on the floor, propped against one of the legs of the desk. If only he could go on sitting there, lost in his memories, maybe even dropping off to sleep, dissolving into the past, quietly disappearing. If it hadn't been for that smell. Schepp turned away from the sun; since his operation he hadn't been able to tolerate bright light. He moved around the desk without rising from the floor. He was now looking at Doro's legs, the kimono hanging down below her knees. Almost at once he was wide awake and slid closer. Looked at Doro's swollen calf. Oh no, how fast it was changing, marbled in shades of pale violet; she would have hated that. Schepp groped in her direction, finally grasped one of her legs, then pressed cautiously with his other hand, trying to banish the ugly marks of *livor mortis* from her calf; that was its name, wasn't it, *livor mortis*, discolouration after death. But where to make the marks go? First he tried upwards, then he pressed down equally towards her slipper. There was a dull sound. Alarmed, Schepp hit his head and saw Doro's hand dangling in front of him. This was too much. He took the hand and held it firmly until it stopped moving, until he had calmed down. Held it as he had held it twenty-nine years ago, as he had promised he would if the worst happened. Now at last he was doing just that.

'I'm here with you,' he promised Doro's hand tenderly. 'I'm holding you tight. Even if you can't feel it any more, we'll get through this.'

A while later he was standing beside her, moved to tears by his own solemnity, and placing her left arm back on the desk. However, it immediately slipped off again. First Schepp had to straighten Doro's torso. That was difficult; it was almost impossible to correct the angle of her throat and neck. But though he had to push and pull quite hard, he tried to comfort himself with the thought that he was helping Doro, even with these pitiful efforts – just as she would help him one day. From now on she would wait for him on the shore of the lake, ready to offer him her energetic little hand as soon as he found himself there with her. On their wedding day she had told him she would do for him exactly what he had said he would do for her.

If *she* were the first to die, she said, she would wait there for him; it would be better to go together, whatever happened, much better.

She had renewed that promise on all of their wedding anniversaries, and although Schepp was as sceptical as ever about the existence of the lake and all the rest of it, he did not express his doubts, and indeed saw the promise as reassurance that their marriage would last for ever.

Curiously enough, today Doro's idea of the next world did not seem to him at all ridiculous but perfectly credible, indeed consoling. He was glad he could cherish one last hope of seeing her again. A lake was better than nothing. How frail she looked! Only now did it strike Schepp that she could no longer disguise her frailty with the radiant smile he had always loved. She sat in his desk chair like a porcelain doll, her nose a little sharper than usual, her cheeks visibly paler, as pale as – Schepp couldn't help thinking of the new waitress, the look she had given him when he had settled his bill the previous night, and her captivatingly pale face.

He forced himself to turn his full attention to his wife. She had become a little less familiar with no colour in her cheeks. Having said that, even during her lifetime she had somehow always been distant and strange in spite of her daily presence. Perhaps because of his middle-class origins, which made him ill at ease in an eight-room apartment with such elegant furnishings. Or perhaps because of her ikebana flower-arranging sessions and her meditative silences. She talked to plants and engaged with objects in her mind; her intuitive nature was not only quick to understand human relationships but also went straight to the heart of the inanimate world. Everything whispered its meaning to her, a meaning that eluded Schepp, meticulous philologist though he was.

For him, her attraction probably lay in that very attitude. She did not need cheerful company, she was in constant touch with things both higher and more profound. Bringing up the children, looking after a rather remote freelance Sinologist, seemed to be all that linked her to the pitiful world this side of the grave. In the evenings she usually sought the company of the I Ching, equipping herself for the challenges of the future, no doubt also of the next world. Before every important decision she sought the advice of the ancient signs. Usually the outcome was good. However, as the years passed she had become ever quieter, more fragile, almost transparent. She did not often smile at Schepp, or take him in her arms to tell him about the cold, dark lake. Or was that just her way of avoiding the conversations that a husband and wife should really have? Schepp could never again touch the heart of her life's secret, as he had on that day when, faced with an isle of the dead, their lives had been decided. Admittedly he had at best a very vague idea of the nature of Doro's fear of the next world. Probably because as a man who did not know much about mysticism he was bound to ask the wrong questions, inevitably conveying some of his own slight distaste, or the derision that would be hard for him to suppress, or his categorical doubts. And of course Doro sensed that. At least, she never tried to discuss the matter with him.

How different she was when it came to praising or criticizing his essays and papers! Schepp glanced across the top of the desk, lingering where there was nothing, now, between Doro's hands but a dark mark on the leather surface – and then he remembered what it was that he wanted to do. He found the manuscript, with the final page added by Doro on top. Sorting through it quickly, he glanced over her notes in the margins and between the lines without really understanding them. At last he had all the sheets in the correct order, with Doro's closing comments at the bottom of the pile. He could begin reading.

But that was impossible. Who could read in this situation, beginning at the beginning, reading every word? There was also the fact that the pages began with his own text, the work he had surely discarded long since. It was absurd. Schepp kept looking through them again and again, at the place where Doro's closing comments began – how familiar her writing was! At least there was that to cling to.

But as soon as he began dipping into the manuscript, the sight of her handwriting made him feel perplexed. Increasingly uneasy, then downright discontented. How could he bear to read what she had written on that final page? Doro had probably not been responsible for her own actions so close to the end. Schepp put that sheet aside quickly, but his eyes lingered on another one of the last pages: 'I am under some pressure, because I must finish this farewell letter tomorrow.' Oh God, what had she been intending to do? Did she realize that her own death was imminent? Or, as she wrote what she wrote, had she even – even anticipated it, gone to meet it? No, out of the question, Doro would never have done such a thing.

Or would she?

That morning, Schepp reluctantly turned back into what he had been all his life, a patient interpreter of primary sources. At the end of his typescript, Doro's notes began with a question mark in the margin, and on the back of the final sheet she had written an abrupt 'As if he would have said such a thing in that situation'. Within the text she had crossed out the name of a bar and substituted the name of his local. What was the point of that? Equally puzzling was the marginal question mark nearer the beginning: 'Why not just call him Hinrich and be done with it?' Schepp leafed through to the conclusion again. 'You and I know that's not the end of the story.' Good heavens, it sounded as if he would have done better not to read it at all.

But to take the comments in at a glance was impossible. He had to read the entire manuscript. Read it from the beginning, or it would be far more difficult to endure. And he really wanted to know, for now he was feeling angry, reproaching Doro, and at the same time he was horrified by the strength of the anger building up inside him. There should be no rancour, no harsh words in the face of death. There must be a misunderstanding. He only needed to read the manuscript from the beginning, then Doro's final lines would surely make sense. Yes, now Schepp really did want to know what she had intended to discuss with him, and why she had chosen this particular manuscript, one he had never shown her because ... because he had decided it was a miserable failure and resolved not to pursue his ambitions to write fiction. He had never regretted the decision, or he would hardly have become the authority he undoubtedly was among Sinologists. Very well, so the novel he had tried to write back then, *Marek the Drunkard*, had come to such a hopeless dead end on page twelve that he had had no idea how to continue, and he had abandoned it. Only to add a few more wild, frantic scenes which he then destroyed immediately out of embarrassment, or at least he had tucked them away somewhere safe.

Marek the Drunkard. No sooner had Schepp begun reading at last, beginning with the first line, than he noticed that he was not really concentrating. At first he read as if in a trance, instantly forgetting each word. Then he skipped entire scenes, not wanting to linger line by line over a manuscript he had picked up only because of Doro's final comments, wishing still less to dwell on her detailed deletions, rephrasings and additions. The church clock struck twelve. He perceived the sound like an admonition to devote himself to reading the pages with the gravity they required. Shafts of sunlight shone into the room. He saw the motes dancing in them. Schepp now stood at the tall reading desk at the far end of the room, where the light was noticeably more muted. He shifted his gaze wearily to the back of Doro's head, her black and silver shock of hair falling over the chair-back, and noticed a fly circling in the air. With some effort he moved and shooed it away.

His gaze passed over the gladioli to the *chaise-longue*, and he remembered how, in the early years of their marriage, Doro would often lie there reading while he worked at the desk, both absorbed in their separate occupations yet not alone. This arrangement struck him as ideal for the situation in which he found himself.

It was not easy to lift Doro out of the chair. Her shoulders were already stiff, while the rest of her was so limp that she kept slipping from his grasp. When he had finally got a firm hold on her he felt the dampness of her kimono; the fabric around her hips was soaked. But he managed to downplay the awkwardness of this through assiduity – Doro lay so light in his arms, so light.

When he had laid her on the *chaise-longue* a little sigh escaped her, which terrified him. Would she suddenly open her eyes? He so hoped she would that the idea almost frightened him. He even held his breath, but Doro remained motionless. The marks of *livor mortis* on her forearms were large now, you couldn't miss them; good thing the kimono had sleeves to cover them.

Schepp was gasping for breath. Schepp had things to do – suddenly everything seemed important. Once he had managed to fold Doro's hands – they eluded him and came apart again and again, until (I'm sorry, Doro, I don't want to hurt you, you're being so difficult today), until he finally forced them to grasp each other – and once he had put a cushion under her neck, she lay there, the familiar filigree figure. He did not dare to straighten the corners of her mouth, he did not dare to press her jaw shut, and he definitely did not dare to close her eyes. He covered her small, stubbornly twisted body – when had he seen it as closely as this during the last few years? – up to the shoulders with a light throw so that she would not be cold.

Now he felt better, now she would be pleased with him. He pushed back a silvery strand of hair from her forehead and buried his head in the hollow of her throat. Hadn't he been wanting to do that for a long time? He pressed his lips to her cold skin just where his favourite mole lay on the other side of her neck. One last time, he considered and rejected the idea of calling a doctor – if he had failed Doro at the moment of death, he would at least keep vigil beside her. If he sat down here and now with the manuscript he could at least share her last hours in retrospect.

He sat on the edge of the *chaise-longue*, carefully sliding a little further back, then a little further back again, pushing Doro's legs up against the upholstery. For a while the fly buzzed somewhere or other, then silence returned and with it came a sense of space, as if the things all around were moving further away from him, right back to the walls. Schepp was sitting beside his wife and amidst that great silence. Now finally he could read in peace.

No one knew whether Marek had been a heavy drinker before Hanni started waitressing and drove us all crazy, every last one of us. Judging by what we heard about him at the Blaue Maus, seems highly unlikely. After all, he lived in a 2CV Dolly delivery van, on the move practically the whole time, and had to watch how much he drank. The cool thing was, he had a water container on the roof of the Dolly. A pipe ran down from the container into a sawn-off aluminium bread bin welded into the wheel housing. That was his wash basin. Imagine that! He liked to park at night in alleys or backyards where the coppers wouldn't roust him out in a hurry – a guy like that very likely couldn't even show an official document saying he was unemployed, no fixed abode neither, you can bet the coppers would've liked to put him behind bars. His long hair, torn old army surplus jacket, patched jeans didn't help either – typical dropout, just the sort the law likes to take in for a body search. On the other hand, although we couldn't really believe it, on the other hand Marek, of all people, claimed to be engaged to be married, and when he showed his narrow gold ring with an inscription inside, *PETRA – Let's do it – 12.4.1971*, we all had to admit that it was serious, I mean more than a whole year, incredible length of time!

The following evening, again, we couldn't believe it. Marek, secretly and deep down – a bourgeois? However this ominous fiancée of his, who none of us had ever seen, had gone off to Greece without him to some island to be an au pair? Wolfi told us, being the manager here, spreading rumours at the bar was kind of his duty. You got so many rumours about Marek that we eventually gave up asking questions and believed anything of him. Apparently his parents came over from some eastern country. Apparently he was a petrolhead and good at tinkering with stuff. Apparently he drove all the way home from Athens with a broken clutch cable, changed gear just by listening, got a great reputation with some of us that way. Not with the girls, though. Not the ladies, at least not with Hanni. She laughed at him outright when she brought him another beer, 'There you go, pet, no laying it on too thick!' While with Big Jörn, who always made a palaver out of putting her tip where she least expected it, with Big Jörn she used to thank him with a cheeky, 'So I guess that gets you a night with me'. Which Marek of course heard, even if he pretended he was too busy rolling a fag.

Actually we didn't know much about him, he didn't say much himself. He only talked about his Dolly. How he bought it with the rusty floor and no MOT certificate and all for 250 marks. How he fell more in love with it every time he hand-picked a spare part for it off a scrap heap and built it in. And how he finally painted the Dolly bright red with a roller. Always something to be welded, greased, cleaned, like in any household, he said. He also claimed that now his Dolly not only featured a proper mattress, 120 by 180 centimetres, but also a duvet, a spirit cooker, a whole lot of candlesticks, oh yes, and the wash basin had an outlet, he had all he needed. Wasn't so good on rainy days when he was in the middle of town, he said, everything getting wet, you had to shit in a bucket too. On those days you were glad to get into bed, and then …? Well, what he did then we'd no idea, some claimed he wrote poetry, maybe he read or listened to Jimi Hendrix on his fifty-watt speakers that he'd built in even before the heater and the cooker.

Or maybe he just lay there and thought of Hanni. In which activity, God knows, like I said, he was not alone. The Blaue Maus had always been a great place to crash out, known for it all over town, round about midnight everyone who'd already had a skinful somewhere else was there, ready to make a night of it. But then Hanni came as waitress – as matey with everyone as if she was another guy. And the way she went around in cut-off jeans, T-shirts much too small for her, that didn't make things any better. She'd push her way through the customers, teasing them while she served the drinks – 'Fancy a nibble with that?' – and if someone tried getting back at her, with her freckles and her bold way, making insinuating advances, she'd send him packing, throwing the guy out herself. 'Is his big brother here too? He'd better leave as well.' That on its own was worth a visit to the Maus for all of us.

Life at the Maus was never boring. What with the place being full of alcoholics, jazz trumpeters, philosophers and other such colourful figures, and from two or three in the morning everyone talking to everyone else across tables and up and down the entire bar. In case of doubt there was always Mutt. Because Hanni, as cheerily as she joked, cursed or knocked back tequilas, was basically the opposite of flirtatious. If someone made the slightest move behind her back, suggesting never mind the pretzels and peanuts, he could fancy nibbling something very different, she'd immediately swing round, brown eyes with all those tiny gold flecks in them putting on a fireworks display, hand on her hip, asking so as we could all hear, 'Who was it wanted a nibble, then?' And when someone had ordered nuts or cigarettes, reckoning he was in with a serious chance, he'd often take his disappointment out on Mutt, Hanni's dog, a mongrel who regularly hung out with us. Did the old boy know who the kicks he often got under the table at dawn were really meant for?

Hanni. Acting so matey and on a level with everyone meant she shielded herself from any problems. Seemed like she didn't much care for men. Big Jörn, who late at night would behave as if he could have her at the drop of a hat, couldn't even provoke her into contradicting his claims. As for Marek, the sort who admired her from afar, she mocked him: 'Still a bit wet behind the ears, are we?' But he had his devious way of getting closer to her. Through Mutt. Marek treated the dog with particular respect, like an old gentleman. When everything was open-ended chaos around four or five in the morning, he'd move close to the dog to protect him from the worst.

Most of all Mutt had to be protected from Big Jörn. Jörn liked firewater, gave you 'smooth body juices and a pure complexion', he said. When he'd tipped enough of it down his throat to set light to his nerve endings he'd go up in flames, all for Hanni, of course. Then Marek just shrugged and took himself off to a quieter corner. There he sat, didn't get much joy in the corner either, couldn't join in the conversation like ours at the bar, just automatically raised his glass when the time seemed right. Couldn't really get real friends that way. Meanwhile Big Jörn was full of drunk boasting: Hanni, let me tell you, what a live wire, you never know if she's going to laugh or bite. So when he said that and more of the same, the only thing Hanni would do is pause in front of him flashing her eyes to shut him up. Those nights Mutt usually suffered a lot.

It could have gone on like this for years. But it all changed one hot, humid July night. 'Love Like a Man' had been playing for some time, it was Wolfi's habitual chucking-out number. But as usual it was only him who set off home, leaving the field to Hanni. And us. Big Jörn really got into his stride on such nights. Entertained the whole Maus with his boastful stories, spiked with racy little details. Stood a round. Firewater for everyone. Every time Marek had to raise his glass to him you can bet he was thinking, the hell with you. 'Another little one won't hurt,' Big Jörn announced, launching into praise for Hanni's charms – if looks could kill he'd have died several times over. But she said nothing, at most just flashed her eyes, and still no one knew whether Big Jörn was her boyfriend, her ex-boyfriend or just showing off. We wanted him to verify his claims. Now Big Jörn had a reputation to lose. So he reached for Hanni just as she was trying to steer past him with a tray of empty glasses, and, while we were still scattering from their clinking and clattering, he laid her down on the bar and gave her a kiss in front of us all.

But not a nice sort of kiss.

The other sort.

He finally lets her go with a triumphant grin. Hanni is breathing heavily, then she starts screaming. Now we all know what to think, and the next moment there's a right old punch-up going on, a real clattering and clanking, and all together we throw Big Jörn out into the street. There Hanni gives him a ringing slap. And just as he's about to get up and scram, Mutt shoots out of the bar barking and snaps at his trouser legs. For a moment Big Jörn glares at the dog, then sends him flying against the wall with a hearty kick. Now everyone would like to kick the shit out of Big Jörn, every last one of us. But while we still stand, gaping, only Marek – Marek of all people, who'd been hanging back until now – first he goes over to Mutt, who's writhing about whining, then without a word he goes up to Big Jörn and smashes his nose in. You should've seen it! Big Jörn howls, there's blood running through his fingers and down his neck, and off he runs.

Next day no one's waiting tables in the Blaue Maus. After much questioning we find out from Wolfi that he's seen this coming right from the beginning, it couldn't end well, a girl who carries on with the customers has no place here. Now what? Now nothing. Still nothing the next evening and the next one. When we threaten to go and drink wherever Hanni turns up if he doesn't take her back of his own free will, Wolfi assures us that he'd rather go bust. But it's not her fault, says none other than Marek, suddenly raising his voice and

Schepp had managed to read up to this point in spite of Doro's corrections, at first with sceptical curiosity, then with horror, finally with mounting anger. At the beginning she had just scored one or two sets of double lines in the margin to draw attention to something, followed by an exclamation or a question mark – he knew her annotation style well enough to understand what she meant. But soon the marginal notes became more extensive, forthright, cutting. Doro had always been a model of discretion, but now that the sharp tone of her comments was unmitigated by lenience, she sparkled with icy elegance. Did she want to make him feel inferior? How was he to take it when she, of all people, told him in the margin what she thought Marek was really doing when the text said expressly that he was just lying there thinking of Hanni? Schepp was embarrassed. In the next section wasn't she openly criticizing not only his protagonist but him, the author, for being inhibited

– why did he keep beating about the bush, circling around the subject? Had he never had a little nibble of someone himself? And when Big Jörn got into his stride, once again there was the remark, 'Oh, why not call him Hinrich and be done with it?' On the back of the sheet, however, she had written, 'Your admiration for him is ridiculous.'

Schepp was extremely annoyed. The solemn mood in which he had wanted to say his last goodbye to Doro was gone. Being dead means no one can answer you back, he snorted at her. But it was her next correction that cut him to the quick. The manuscript slipped from his hands, he got up and looked around him, at a loss. Then he started pacing back and forth, beating time in the air with his index and little fingers to the rhythm of the retorts bursting out of him.

What had put him in such a rage, what had him pacing back and forth in full lecturing mode, was a single tiny pen stroke. At the place where Marek spoke up for the first time, Doro had crossed out the name Hanni and written 'Dana' over it. The louder Schepp's heels tapped the wooden floor, the more baffled he felt. As soon as he had convinced himself that Doro had chosen that name at random, it struck him, however, that this could be no coincidence. She had come looking for him, hadn't she, one evening maybe four years ago, in La Pfiff; she'd seen Dana, even spoken briefly to her. Or had it been five years ago? But what would a girl called Dana, might he ask, have to do with *Marek the Drunkard*? The only parallel with Hanni being that Dana had been a waitress too – although decades later!

Schepp stopped in the doorway through which he had come to begin the day what now seemed an eternity ago. He breathed deeply, in and out, until he thought, again, that Doro must have forgotten to change the water in the vase. With every breath the silence came closer, creeping towards him from the far end of the room. Eventually it once again embraced him entirely.

But this was a different kind of silence. Schepp stood there listening to what was in his mind. Or outside of his mind? For a while he heard a buzzing, sometimes closer, sometimes further away, as if it were a part of the silence. Only when the sound stopped did he remember what was causing it. He stepped across the wooden floor as warily as a man about to commit murder, reached the *chaise-longue*, saw the fly sitting on Doro's eye just where the lids met at a sharp angle. He could hardly swat it while it was there. Where did a fly come from anyway at this time of year; shouldn't it be dead by now? Only when he was almost touching it could he shoo it away.

Schepp's glance lingered on the little slits of Doro's eyes, moved to the bridge of her nose, which was sticking up in the air, to her lower jaw hanging so inelegantly open. How could he close it without hurting her? All at once he was back to loving her as much as ever; there would be time to quarrel later. Schepp knelt down in front of Doro and looked closely into her open mouth. He could see nothing in that dark space.

He inhaled the smell of death and shuddered at the thought that she would leave her jaws open like that for ever and ever.

How exactly did *rigor mortis* work?

The fermentation of bodily fluids, decomposition, decay?

He didn't want to think about it.

'All right, Doro,' he said hesitantly, raising his voice, 'if you're going to start about Dana then please take things in their proper order.'

Even when the children were still at home, and he was glad to get an hour or two in the evenings to devote to the heroic tales of the Tang dynasty or the brushstrokes of Song calligraphy, Doro had sometimes, surprisingly, come back out of her bedroom and over to him at his desk to – well, to say or do what? He had never known what to make of it, and if he asked her for an explanation she quite often went away looking offended. As if she had wanted to bring him out of his shell. Yet these kind of approaches had never been helpful. You have to tackle difficulties head on, systematically, and what use was it now – Schepp was back in the full flow of his perorations, once again speaking emphatically and clearly like a tutor lecturing a difficult examination candidate – what use was it now to drop Dana's name at the very first opportunity and then abandon him with it? Things have to make sense before they can be cleared up, right?

The Dana business was long ago and forgotten now. Still, at the very least, you should begin at the beginning to leave no room for doubt. And anyway, this wasn't how he had imagined their farewell, so full of misunderstandings. The beginning had certainly been his operation. No, actually it had all started in his childhood. Even at the age of five he spent most of his time with books, his glasses would have only got in the way playing football. Yes, it had all started in his childhood, which had consisted mostly of being teased. At least he couldn't be beaten up; he was so short-sighted that he was thought unable to defend himself, almost on a par with a girl. And if it hadn't started in his childhood then definitely in his youth, a time of renunciation. Where his contemporaries succeeded, he stood aside. Luckily the details eluded him because he saw anything that was more than three to five metres away only in indistinct outline. Of course he noticed that something was going on. He just didn't let on, learned another language instead. And although at university he was at last considered a genius and quietly admired, he still always had to stand aside when the real prizes were handed out.

Admittedly his tranquil life as a research fellow rather than a university professor had its advantages; he didn't have to bother with feminist Sinology, or modern business Chinese or even online-chat Chinese, all ghastly prospects for a committed scholar like him, devoted to the study of primary sources. You could escape such horrors only by burying yourself in the ancient texts. Nevertheless he had loved life in his own guarded way, and after all he had been lucky once. Although looking back he couldn't understand why a woman like Dorothee Wilhelmine Renate, Countess von Hagelstein had chosen him. Then, in the summer of 2003, after more than two wonderful peaceful decades with her, on his doctor's advice, he had laser surgery on his eyes. Whereupon the tranquillity ended.

It was terrible to see the world in such detail, so sharply outlined, all of a sudden! It had always been so comfortably impersonal in its remote milkiness; Schepp hadn't felt he was missing anything. Now it dazzled him with a confusingly large number of details – could someone like Doro, who had never had any problems with her eyes, ever have imagined that? Overnight his life seemed like one long missed opportunity. If he had previously renounced a great deal, never complained, he was now determined to make up for it. Schepp developed a need for other people which he had never believed possible. He wanted to participate in just about everything, at least as a spectator. And because of all these needs and wants, peace of mind became a thing of the past.

First he encountered afresh his hand-picked coterie of students. Then he realized that it was possible to go to a nearby bar or café after seminars to continue their conversations in a more informal setting, and to develop relationships. Oh, Schepp was so curious about everything and everyone. He was as hungry for the world as if anything that had satisfied him before no longer counted. As if he had to reinvent himself from scratch and prove himself like a man who had no more excuses left. Not that he had serious ambitions, heaven forbid! But to be open and receptive to everything that previously had been out of sight, out of reach – up to a point, of course; after all, Schepp was married – well, to be receptive to everything there was to be seen and perhaps studied more closely, he should expect that of himself, shouldn't he?

Then came a hot, humid July evening. The unworldly scholar had turned into a positive charmer and in the protective circle of his students had become familiar with the few bars around the Free

University campus. A PhD student had suggested the dimly lit La Pfiff because it was delightfully empty. This is the moment when Dana appears in the picture, although at the time of course no one knew her name; she was merely an unknown woman standing at the bar. At first glance a woman in a trouser suit, everything about her luxurious, accompanied by a gentleman and another lady. At second glance a woman with short hair neatly parted, strikingly pale skin, alarmingly large eye sockets with weary dark eyes. When she turned her bony face with its prominent cheekbones towards the man on her left or the lady on her right, that was sufficiently exciting for a man like Schepp.

And then suddenly he saw her in the arms of the man – no, really the man was in hers – he was unable to fend her off. Schepp drained his glass of red wine in a single swallow. His PhD students could discuss what they liked, he had eyes only for the unknown woman. She surely was going to kiss the man right into the ground any moment now. Then she calmly raised her right leg – or was it her left leg? Made no difference – and wrapped it around his hips, drawing him closer, her tongue working in his mouth unabated as if she wanted to devour him there and then. The next moment, however, she was pushing him away, turning from him to the lady, who had been watching with interest, and smiling.

That ought to have been enough for one evening.
But then came the kiss between the two women!
At first Schepp was sure his eyes must be deceiving
him when he saw the unknown woman in the arms
of the other lady, whom she did not just allow to
kiss her – by now he really couldn't believe his eyes
– oh no! The lady bit the unknown woman's neck.
When she finally moved away, Schepp saw a mark
on the skin. A dark blue tattoo the size of an one-
euro coin. A few moments later they were all three
standing at the bar as if nothing had happened.
Schepp's mouth was dry. For the rest of the evening
he couldn't help looking over at them frequently,
especially at the alluring unknown woman. Soon
he was certain about the sign. It sat right over one
of the tendons at her throat, small enough to move
every time she turned her head, and she turned her
head frequently.

Just once that evening her eyes met his, staring
him down, forcing him to look away – what a
humiliation – before they went on scanning the
room. When she finally left with the other two,
heading out into a night seemingly so vast that
Schepp felt he could see the stars sparkling from
where he sat, she passed close to him, and at
last he could recognize the sign on her neck, a
Chinese character. As he tried to decipher it, he
almost became frightened, for he realized that
he had seen it often, but where? The curve of the

brushstroke was familiar, although it had not been elegantly executed as a tattoo; it was the sign for … what? Schepp mopped his forehead with his handkerchief. It took him some time to realize that such a coincidence was not the work of Fate, least of all deliberately arranged for him. And that he too could go home now.

After that he dreamt of the sign at night. When Doro regarded him inquiringly during the day he looked down at the floor, ashamed. What could he have said to her? That evening an extraordinary thing had occurred in his life, a life that so far had known only an extraordinary absence of experience. From then on he kept a frequent eye on the scene of this event to see if there would be a sequel. Oh, he had no ambitions of his own; it would only have been a case of looking, of participating in something he imagined as the simultaneous height of depravity and of bliss.

The devotion he had always received at home now became almost like a burden. He avoided it as much as he could. Yet it was Doro who solved the puzzle of the tattoo: as he sat in her room one afternoon at their usual time with a pot of green tea, his eye fell on the sign quite by chance. There it was among the other sixty-three signs of the I Ching; Doro had hung them on the wall here as well. Schepp stood right in front it; he couldn't possibly miss it. How beautiful it was when written by a master of calligraphy! He immediately asked Doro whether he could borrow one of her commentaries, if possible the Southern Commentaries, if she could spare the book. Doro raised an eyebrow in surprise. But how could he have explained himself?

Having found the sign and studied it almost daily, his peace of mind was definitely gone. The unknown woman, however, stood him up evening after evening, though he became a regular at the bar, exchanging banter with this or that member of the staff. Paul, the manager, a jovial soul in his late forties with a well-tended moustache, known to everyone as Paulus, would greet him with, 'Evening, Professor, doing okay, are we?' Paulus spent most of the evening behind the bar, an equable presence washing up glasses as if the goings-on were beneath his notice. La Pfiff was not plugged into the cultured bohemian milieu of the digital age; customers came in and either backed straight out again or didn't leave until hours later. By midnight everyone had both argued and fraternized with everyone else. In his own fashion, anyway, Schepp became part of it.

It was useful that La Pfiff was within walking distance of his apartment. The regular course of his days now gave way to an irregularity that in the end became routine, although it was the opposite of the former kind. Hitherto a man of the old school who combed his remaining hair over his bald patch and vacillated between melancholy and megalomania, Schepp took to shaving his head, chose colourful handkerchiefs for his breast pocket, bought stronger aftershave, gained a certain authority with the occasional clever quibble that earned him a laugh – oh, he was tired of his reasonable mind. He hardly did any research; soon he wasn't even publishing, and there was an admixture of mockery in the respectful empathy he now encountered from his full-time colleagues at the University. He once even overheard someone calling him Professor Unrat, after the nickname – Professor Garbage – of Professor Raat, the protagonist of Heinrich Mann's novel. What did PhD students know about anything anyway? He also, and for the first time, offered an introductory course on the I Ching, much to the surprise of Doro, whom he now only ever saw when they drank tea together in the afternoon.

It could probably have gone on like this for ever. But then she reappeared – the woman of whom he thought every day with a shiver of admiration. Schepp had long given up any hope of seeing her again, but when he entered La Pfiff one evening he almost stumbled into her. There was no doubt, it was definitely her. With that Chinese character tattooed on her throat she was unmistakably branded. For a Sinologist, that was not a coincidence, but had been arranged by Fate especially for him, the only one there who understood the sign. She was standing at the bar with a tray in her hands on which Paulus was placing a round of drinks. She had come back.

This time to work as a waitress.

Her name was Dana, and she was from Poland 'or somewhere in the east'. Paulus knew almost nothing about her. No, he couldn't remember ever having seen her at La Pfiff before. Or if he did he wasn't saying, and Schepp was careful not to mention it. For the rest of the evening he watched her as casually as he could; he was bound to glance at a new waitress now and then. Once more their eyes met briefly, once more hers rested on him without any interest. When she served him she even asked the same question she had asked at the table next to his:

Where had a nice lad like him left his girlfriend this evening?

Schepp gulped down the contents of his glass so that he could order another drink quickly. This time he asked her straight out about her tattoo, saying he had seen her here in the summer, he was certain that he knew her.

In her charming accent Dana replied that she knew him and his sort too, and particularly that trick; he'd have to think up something subtler.

'Oh, please!' objected Schepp. It wasn't like that at all, as a Sinologist he must protest, he'd have known a sign like the one on her neck with his eyes closed! He would in fact have liked to have leapt to his feet and bitten her right on that spot. He didn't say that, of course. Instead he asked whether she knew what a fateful mark she was carrying, an oracular pronouncement of which Kung Tze himself had said –

This was *too* subtle for her, said Dana, turning away.

Schepp sat there red-faced for the rest of the evening, not sure whether he should feel more offended as a man or as an academic. Even now, years later, he was overcome by embarrassment when he conjured up the scene; he ought really to have given Dana a slap in the face there and then, and that would have been that. Especially when he thought of her scent, some cheap Polish perfume that gave her an improper air, as if both the perfume and the woman were cheap and available.

He shook himself, pulled a face, as if his room, too, were full of Dana's objectionable perfume. He certainly wasn't going to think about that today. It was highly unsuitable, and damn it all, he had thought of that woman Dana far too often, thought of her every day. Every night. Well? Did that make him a worse human being, a worse husband; hadn't he always lavished care and attention on Doro? Although, even so, it was a long time, yes, a very long time since he had actually touched her.

Good God, it happened to so many men, it didn't have to mean anything.

Schepp forced himself back to the present. How long had he been kneeling in front of Doro? I always loved you, you know I did.

But you don't know about Dana, he thought, getting up with difficulty. His knees hurt. He stepped away from Doro and the *chaise-longue*. He had always thought that she had known nothing about all that, nothing at all. And in actual fact it really hadn't been anything more than a few rather unseemly passing thoughts. Why had he lapsed into thinking about Dana today, anyway? Shaking his head, Schepp set off along the fishbone pattern of the parquet. How could he be recalling such a person in the presence of death? How she repelled him in retrospect, how he despised her, how he hated her!

His right hand beat time in the air to his muttered exclamations of annoyance, index and little fingers extended, the rest of his hand clenched into a fist. Until he remembered why he had thought of Dana, whereupon his hand stopped in mid-air and dropped powerlessly to his side. It was Doro's own fault! There was a sudden rushing in his ears as if the ground were about to give way beneath him. As he clung to his desk, however, his sense of equilibrium was restored. After he had said out loud several times that Dana was really,

really entirely different from Hanni, you could almost say her opposite – surely that was obvious, he hoped that showed once and for all how absurd Doro's corrections were – he remembered what his initial intention had been. Wasn't he going to keep a vigil at Doro's side? Wasn't this his chance to read her final message? He had to continue the reading, never mind Hanni, never mind Dana.

He returned to the *chaise-longue*, picked up the sheets of paper from the floor and put them in order. He looked for that passage with Marek, the scene in which he spoke up to defend – no, not Dana – to defend Hanni. Schepp decided to ignore that comment in the margin, even though Doro had stuck to it consistently, crossing out Hanni's name every time and changing it to Dana's. It was no use, he had promised her to read the manuscript.

Next day there's no one waiting tables in the Blaue Maus. After much questioning we find out from Wolfi that he's seen this coming from the beginning, it couldn't end well, a girl who carries on with the customers has no place here. Now what? Now nothing. Still nothing the next evening and the next one. When we threaten to go and drink wherever Hanni turns up if he doesn't take her back of his own free will, Wolfi assures us that he'd rather go bust. But it's not her fault, says none other than Marek, raising his voice and pointing at

Big Jörn, who has actually dared to turn up again and who's grinning broadly at all of us with a big plaster on his nose. He's the one who ought to be banned from this bar, not Hanni.

Almost two weeks went by, and whatever we said Wolfi stuck to his guns, pointing out the damage that had been done. But then one day Marek takes his savings passbook out of his jacket and shoves it over to him, asking him to see if the sum in it comes to enough. Wolfi pulls back his ponytail, looking awkward. We all crowd round, we say what a good lad young Marek is, we urge Wolfi to get a grip, we say we'll contribute too if necessary. But it's enough.

Okay, says Wolfi, sweeping the passbook off the bar, he's no monster. He lifts the telephone receiver and hands it to the surprised Marek. As a reward he can give her the good news himself.

Much laughter. We all raise our glasses to Marek, our saviour, and tell him to have courage.

Then what? In his excitement Marek can hardly find the right holes in the dial for all the numbers Wolfi dictates out of a notebook, Wolfi has to write them down on an order pad. Then the phone is answered. He stammers a bit and says, 'It's the Blaue Maus here,' words which are hailed raucously even at the tables furthest back. Marek now has to shout to make himself heard. Everything's topsy-turvy here, he says, she can hear that for herself,

Wolfi urgently needs reinforcements, this evening would be best or at least starting tomorrow, she's missed a lot. Later he claims he didn't say the last bit, but all of us crowding round him, we all of us heard it. To our other questions he replies with a silent nod. We take it as a good sign, we pat him on the back, we buy him a drink. And so it goes for the rest of the evening until Marek's completely pissed. Only Big Jörn sneers and says he doesn't know what's up with us all of a sudden. That girl Hanni is 'totally crazy, totally frigid', he claims, she only does it 'with other dykes'. And on and on until he's thrown out again, this time by Wolfi.

Next day Hanni's back, waitressing like she's never been away. She thanks Marek by ignoring him while letting anyone else raise his glass to her and buy her a tequila. Although Mutt is safe amongst all this turmoil, Marek sees to him regularly, making sure he's okay. Only when dawn breaks and most people have left does Hanni approach him. Instead of cashing up, she bends right over him, her silver earring dangling in his face, and whispers to him just loud enough for those of us still there to hear, telling him that – and here he goes rigid with shock, maybe hoping he heard wrong or he's drunk, but no …

'You've earned yourself a night with me,' says Hanni, her brown eyes sparkling with all the little gold flecks in them, not indifferent or joking, dead serious. Imagine that! Marek looks at her, or really he looks through her, he sees her – or doesn't see her – turning away and smiling the way she's only ever smiled at others, never before at him. As if suddenly he wasn't still wet behind the ears.

That night Marek parked in the middle of the traffic island, where he wasn't woken up by the noise of the rush-hour traffic but by the cops. It would be the first of many encounters between him and the Federal authorities, although they never found any illegal substances in his Dolly van. And least of all Hanni, because deep down Marek was afraid that he had misunderstood her and if he approached her to claim his night she'd only laugh at him for being still wet behind the ears. It was the first of many nights he spent avoiding making his claim.

Next evening Hanni was acting outrageously normal, nothing to suggest she'd said that totally incredible thing and magically bound one of the customers to her – or however it was that Marek felt while he waited in silence. Whenever he came in to the Maus we could see how awkward he felt and it got worse when Hanni went over to him. Even if she only said one word to him, he was totally speechless. Overnight everything had changed, everything he saw, heard, thought about here. Poor old Marek, we thought, grinning at him from the bar, the brightest of us analyzing him – sharp as a set of knives, we were. His quiet contentment, the sort that accompanies constant hopeless adoration, had been replaced by simple moodiness, we concluded. Or something along those lines.

Anyway, Marek really set about drinking now; he was the first to arrive in the Maus, and when the buzz and bustle of the place went flat around five in the morning he was the last to order a final beer. But he didn't really enjoy it any more, you could see that, he even developed an overwhelming grudge against Mutt. Some nights he stayed away, and instead – we knew this from Wolfi, as manager he was duty-bound to gossip – he drove around in his Dolly until his eyes closed of their own accord. If he turned up in the Maus again the next evening or the evening after that, he didn't tell us anything. Rumour had it that he did some long-haul driving for various jobs; seems he was doing the lighting for a one-man show and travelled either ahead of or behind it on tour. Someone or other said he'd seen him scavenging on a scrap heap like before; he was painting his red Dolly van black, he didn't answer questions, all he might say, reluctantly, was, 'I'm not doing DIY stuff, I'm working.' Others said … oh, there were so many rumours about Marek that finally we stopped wondering about him.

And what about Hanni? She had better things to do than bother with lads that didn't have a regular job, didn't even have a proper roof over their heads. Autumn came. And winter. When Marek had finished doing up his home by punching a skylight in the roof of the Dolly, he drove off to Greece to see his fiancée, the one he'd been with or rather hadn't been with for a year and a half, probably so that she could sort him out. On the other hand Wolfi claimed that Marek carried Hanni's phone number around all the time like a talisman, and when drunk enough he'd shown it at the bar, so he'd obviously kept it. He said it was simply because he didn't have another jacket, just the one into whose breast pocket he'd put the piece of paper that day.

Perhaps that's why it all worked out so badly for Marek in the end. Anyway he was back from Greece after only three months. Even if he had to drive most of the way on one cylinder, taking gradients against the wind, hair-raising stuff – as we found out later, much later, when we heard the entire story, all the details – and most likely no one but Marek would have made it. In Salzburg the Austrian customs did him over good and proper; Marek was used to that, he happily explained the oil painting that now covered the bonnet, the customs man was so impressed he forgot to inspect the engine.

Then it was his German colleague's turn; the German customs man, however, showed little interest in art but a great deal in Marek's passport, he took it into his cubby-hole, stayed there for a long time, finally came out saying, 'Sorry, you're under arrest.'

This had to be a joke, said Marek, sounding remarkably lively; the customs man asked for his date of birth just to be on the safe side, nodded yes, there was a search warrant out for this very same Marek Seliger. After they'd taken away his belt and his boots they gave him a cell that was, roughly speaking, three times the size of the mattress in his Dolly, the barred window hardly as big as the new skylight. But why, what was it all about? Although they didn't know, they did tell him, shrugging, that matters would take their course, was there anyone he wanted to phone? Then Marek, without stopping to think, put his hand in the breast pocket of his jacket and

For the second time, Schepp had reached a point in his reading where he had to stand up and get some air. He was in such a state that he accused Doro to her face of deliberately distorting the facts, of malicious insinuation. Angrily he asked her why she always had to destroy everything, even in death! Now she had gone and spoilt even this sad day for him, maliciously planning it in advance. He had always, he said, suspected her of, in her quiet way, hatching ideas he'd rather not have known about, of laying plans that then, thank God, she didn't have the courage to put into practice.

Of course he still didn't know what had been on his wife's mind year in, year out, but he guessed. He had bravely read through what started as a series of corrections, but became a second text superimposed on his own. Doro must have had some entirely different intention in mind in retelling the story. Not only had she consistently changed Hanni's name to Dana, she was soon renaming the Blaue Maus La Pfiff, and Wolfi became Paulus at the first opportunity, although in fact she had put Paul, which was officially correct but no one called him that – for two pins Schepp would have got his fountain pen and corrected the correction. In the final passage, on the other hand, where Marek was on the road, in Greece, on the Yugoslavian *autoput* and in jail, Doro started replacing Marek's name as well. There was no bearing it: 'Why not at least call him Hinrich?' she wrote in the margin near where the customs man asked Marek's date of birth, and on the back of the sheet she added, 'You'd always have liked to be a Marek, admit it. Someone who for once in his life plays the man and promptly gets his reward. Whereas all your life you've only been a genius, one who would rather – '

It was at this point that Schepp had got up. What had been gnawing at Doro, that she assumed such things about him? What had made her play him off against Marek, call him a 'hopeless case who had never done anything much in life, and so couldn't have had the faintest hope of finding a Hanni or a Nanni or a Dana or whatever they might be called. Your little daydreams and nocturnal dreams too?' Here Schepp had finally left off reading, had had to get some air. Probably he ought to have given Doro a slap in the face there and then, and that would have been that.

Shaking his head, he looked at her. Had he been wrong about her his entire life? Had she just been pretending all those years?

'That can't be right,' he protested, startled by the certainty of his tone, and he added quietly, 'But I always loved you, didn't I? And don't I love you still? Won't I love you for the rest of my life?'

Then he fell silent again, and it was so quiet that he heard a humming, a familiar and homely sound, he thought. A sudden premonition, a suspicion quickly becoming certainty that perhaps Doro didn't want to be loved by him any longer, grabbed him by the throat. Hell, why had he ever written *Marek the Drunkard*? Why had Doro found the manuscript, why couldn't she think of anything better to do than read it as a disguised version of the affair that, she was insinuating, he'd had with Dana? A character like Marek had nothing, absolutely nothing to do with the married life of Dr Hinrich Schepp, acknowledged as a leading international expert on ancient Chinese script.

As far as he could remember, he had written *Marek the Drunkard* at the beginning of the seventies, basing it vaguely on the story of a college classmate. He had thought it up and put it together in the light of what little he had heard about the man. Schepp had been in his late twenties, an assistant in the department and studying for his doctorate, no Doro or any other woman in the picture. Well, it was probably also the story of the quiet desperation that had crept up on him during those winter evenings of '72, or was it '73? Evenings when he hung around the library until the cleaner threw him out, because the room he rented had no heating. Possibly *Marek the Drunkard* did have a little, a very little, to do with himself, although he had been to the Blaue Maus only once, and until his marriage had been a teetotaller. For Doro simply to equate him with Marek when he neither held a driving licence nor had the money to spend all evening in bars or anywhere else – he couldn't, wouldn't accept that.

On the other hand, and again he felt weak, fragile, on the other hand she could have assumed that the text was new, or written recently, and in that event she was positively *bound* to think that he was writing to get something off his chest, something he had carefully concealed and hushed up in real life. Schepp immediately calmed down again – how could anyone die with such a dreadful mistaken belief? To be dead, he thought, means above all that you can't answer questions, you can't clear things up, you can't get things straight and see that you may have misunderstood them, so they will also be hopelessly false for other people, if they will stay that way. Schepp stood there savouring this idea, which made him feel both mild and melancholy, and if he wasn't to weep aloud and hide, that was how he wanted to feel today. He listened for the humming that had just broken off, even the ensuing silence seemed curiously familiar and yet unimaginably vast. To make room for this vastness everything had moved as far back towards the walls as possible, a gigantic silence in a gigantic room, above a gigantic abyss.

At this point Schepp was almost overcome by desperation concerning his own life, but even before it could unfold completely it had turned into remorse, into the urgent feeling that he should apologize; after all, Doro was not to blame for the confusion she had left behind! It was true that he feared the worst so far as the rest of her corrections were concerned, but it was his own fault, he ought to have told her about *Marek the Drunkard* years, decades, ago, ought to have shown her the manuscript. Maybe they would have read it together and then destroyed it, yes, that would probably have been the best thing to do. Now it was too late. She lay there like someone who finally had discovered something deliberately kept from her, like a woman who would be bound to feel bitter about this last secret she had torn from her married life to take to the grave, at least that was how she must have seen it. Oh Doro. How stupid, how stupid.

Although he was horrified by the power of the *rigor mortis* that had overtaken her – only her torso remained flexible – he nudged her as if to wake her from a bad dream, and although he was also horrified by how cold her body was he kissed her on both cheeks. For a few moments he was not afraid of her any more, he just wanted to warm her and scold her gently, but most of all to be with her. How long had she been lying here, consumed by jealousy and now dead? As if in reply the clock of the Church of the Good Shepherd struck twice. Did that mean it was one-thirty, two-thirty or three-thirty already?

Never mind. He would stay beside her until he began to turn cold and rigid himself. Not thinking anything, not feeling anything – except for her closeness, which of course would continue undiminished even after her death. Schepp imagined Doro standing by that cold, dark lake, waiting for him. For her it would probably be the merest blink of an eye, then eternity would dawn for him as well. They would be reunited, although in death, who knew, perhaps joined more closely than in life. Always supposing she had been right, always supposing there really was a next world. And supposing an atheist could reach it if someone was waiting for him there. And then could do away, as a matter of priority, with every misunderstanding that hadn't been discovered in time here below. Schepp felt positively solemn.

Unfortunately at that very moment he recalled the cardinal error that would have to be cleared up in the next world, the whole story beginning with Marek and perhaps not even ending with Dana, and at the same moment he thought of Doro coming to look for him in La Pfiff years ago and meeting Dana. On an evening that was, at first, like any other, he had been at his usual table beneath the groin-vaulted ceiling and Doro had come through the door like an apparition. You could see at once, from the way she looked, that something had happened; it was surprising enough to see her there all of a sudden – once or twice he had mentioned La Pfiff to her, but never where it was and how you got there.

It had been Pia who had brought her there, Pia's surprising phone call, the news that she was getting a divorce. Doro thought that at least Pia's father could prevent his 'wild, uncontrollable daughter' taking this sudden, rash step; he was to call her straight away, she said, and have 'a firm word'; she herself was at her wits' end. Oh yes, it was the middle of the day in the US, this couldn't be put off, after all a divorce wasn't something you embarked on 'just because you fancied doing it', she hoped there was a telephone in the place?

With these words she had turned to Paulus for help, but before he could find his mobile Dana had brought hers out from beneath her apron. During the entire call with Pia, Schepp had had to watch the two women fall quickly into animated conversation. In the course of which Doro tapped Dana's tattoo several times; finally she gave her some money and they shook hands. Of course the phone call had done nothing to prevent Pia's divorce, he could have told Doro right away that it wouldn't. Pia was as incorrigible as her mother; once she had got something into her head she would go through with it. What came back to him most clearly now, many years later, and seemed a bit strange was the last look that Dana had given Doro, as she had walked away with him – the entire scene had seemed dreadfully embarrassing, everyone in La Pfiff had seen it, and to top it all, that smile Dana gave his wife as she left, one could almost feel jealous! And the way Doro had smiled back! Rather foolishly, he thought now, her entire face shining; normally she hardly perspired at all, but at that moment a light sheen of sweat had appeared on her forehead, her cheeks, even a slight gleam on her upper lip.

Was it possible that Dana had worked the same magic on Doro as on – well, not just on him, the Professor in the corner, oh no! On every man in La Pfiff who had eyes to see. And ears to hear the charming *double entendres* of her jokes. And a nose to pick up the sweet smell that followed her. Once again Schepp's thoughts circled around Dana when he wanted to focus them exclusively on Doro. Dana who had so curtly rejected him – long before Doro's appearance in La Pfiff – when he had spoken to her about the sign at her throat. Even then he had noticed the bold, tarty look of her, and it had only been his injured pride, his pride as a Sinologist, that had made him ask her about it again the following evening …

Did she really know what she was carrying around with her, he inquired zealously. Something rather gloomy, an oracular pronouncement upon which old Kung Tze had commented as follows ….

It was still too subtle for her, Dana had replied, turning away.

This time Schepp didn't sit there red-faced for the rest of the evening, this time he was prepared, and when she went outside to smoke he bought a packet of cigarettes from Paulus and went outside too, hypocritically pretending to need a light.

Was that finally obvious enough?

It soon became clear that Dana had no idea about her Chinese character. It had simply been 'the sexiest' thing she had seen while leafing through the tattoo parlour's catalogue. Schepp told her at length about the I Ching, although he would have preferred to bite her throat quickly, firmly, where she bore the mark of its twenty-ninth character – that is, if he hadn't been a respectable elderly gentleman and, well, happily married. By way of a substitute he did his best to confuse Dana with mysterious allusions to the sign; in his gentle didactic manner he was soon on top form, nodded understandingly even when she asked silly questions, praised her intuitive grasp of the oracle, imagined allegorical elements all over the place, new puzzles that only he (in many future sessions with her) would be able to solve, yes, he was determined to trace all the transformations of the macrocosm on the tendon at her throat, yin and yang, heaven and earth, dark and light, soft and firm, and of course south and north, those were the eternal opposites he revealed to her.

In fact he didn't have much to say. The little he knew from reading Doro's books of commentaries could have been summed up in a couple of sentences. *Kan*, the deep, the abysmal, stood both for a ravine and for the water at the bottom of the ravine; stood for heart, soul, mind; was linked in some way to danger or pointed to danger; and also meant a 'middle son', whoever or whatever that might be – how could a woman like Dana understand that when Schepp didn't understand it himself? A lady-killer of the old school, he gently touched this or that stroke in the complex character of the tattoo with the tip of his forefinger, following the curve as if helping Dana to understand it. Dana's own responses were confined to, 'What a one you are!', 'Fancy you knowing all this, Professor', or the merest mocking look. Yet it was an acknowledged fact that on that evening Schepp became a smoker and her constant companion during her breaks outside.

That didn't mean that she treated him with more familiarity than the other customers; on the contrary, she even seemed to be protecting the sign on the tendon at her throat from him. Although word got around as to who was serving the drinks at La Pfiff these days, and soon the bar was unusually crowded and noisy, Dana walked the aisles past the tables evening after evening unmolested, untouchable. The bar seemed made for her, large enough to display her various talents, small enough for everyone to see what he had been missing – a stage that meant the world to many of the spectators.

Those spectators obeyed her every word; they ate out of her hand, drank whatever she served them, and although something quite different might have been ordered, no one dared respond to her pert remarks. For although Dana cast her spell over everyone with her charm and her slight eastern accent, and even the women turned to look at her, at heart she was the opposite of flirtatious. When one of the customers, a hopeful young man whom they all called Kiddo, began describing her with enthusiasm as the best bad waitress he'd ever come across, she could probably do almost anything, shouldn't they think of her as a kind of minder or nurse instead – well, she whirled round at once and silenced not only him but all the others drinking in the bar. 'Anyone here want to be minded?' she inquired in an undertone, looking so slowly from table to table that everyone felt they'd been caught in some guilty act and devoted themselves to their glasses. But Kiddo, a dubious character of unattractively unwashed appearance with a face inviting a slap and bushy side-whiskers that almost came down to his chin, as if that made him a real man – Kiddo ducked into the crowd standing at the bar and was seen no more that evening.

Schepp registered that with pleasure. His gaze followed Dana while she strode around the room as if shooting from the hip, furious down to the tips of her toes. He didn't yet know that she had an unsuccessful career as a dancer behind her, but he could see it, good God, he could see it. The fact that that career had been a failure, a few short engagements in third-class shows, made no difference when he learnt about it later. He was no wiser on the vital point: had she exerted her obvious talents only to drive men crazy – or women as well? An excitingly terrible idea.

Schepp sat. Schepp drank. Schepp waited. Was he not the only one who knew what Dana was really like? Hadn't he seen it with his own eyes? He was always trying to extract a revelation from her when he followed her outside. He discovered all sorts of things, but not what he was hoping to discover. After a few weeks he knew a good deal about the circumstances of her life, the past circumstances of her life, because she liked to tell him about her childhood with her grandmother in Galicia, and how she had helped out in the fields as a little girl; they'd even had a television, a tractor, there was an uncle in America, in short it had been a golden age – but she was airily elusive so far as her present life was concerned, she reacted to questions both impulsively and confusingly: 'Well, of course, Professor, a bit of fun makes things even more fun.' Was that supposed to mean – ? Was it just naïve chatter, or was there subtle calculation behind it?

Dana. As every single one of his questions led only to more questions, never to a definite answer, Schepp thought her capable of anything. He often found her out in a lie; she was both a talkative and a muddled creature who seemed to have forgotten how a sentence had begun by the time she reached the end of it – her brain was a labyrinth of blind alleys, what she said was surprising, sometimes amusing, but above all a strain on the listener, or at least on a listener like Schepp, who doubted and even despaired of her mind when she talked to him. Until the image of a mobile hanging from the ceiling occurred to him. Yes, he said to himself, that may be how her mind functions, each thought fitted separately to make up a constantly circling structure, moved forwards by the slightest breath of air, next moment backwards or upwards, downwards, something that seemed puzzlingly fickle and unpredictable, but in reality was nothing but a natural process, the outcome of a change in air current rather than thought process.

Soon there was no resisting Dana's erratic way of conversing. It was something of a borderline experience for the honest scholar he had been all his life: he understood that when he talked to her it wasn't the meaning but the sound of the words that mattered. From then on he stopped speaking logically to her, no more arguing, insisting, deploying his brilliance; instead he indulged in a sweet buzz of sound, rhetorically dressing up an absence of meaning. Dana would sometimes smile at him with her big, empty eyes, a reward worth more than any international recognition he had ever received.

He, number one in his field of study, spent an entire spring, almost an entire summer with her, smoking, agreeing with nearly all of her mysteriously wayward remarks as if he had finally found someone who understood his innermost mind. He was entirely absorbed in his new life. Doro at most wrinkled her nose and said nothing. There was nothing worth talking about, was there? The fact that Schepp had discovered the life of bars and red wine and smoking, all in moderation, of course, who could blame him? Certainly not Doro with her gentle sympathy. 'If you ever stop loving me I shall notice at once,' she had assured him when they married, when he had asked her what she expected from their life together and without stopping to think she had replied, 'Nothing.' All she wanted was to be happy. But suppose one day she wasn't? She'd know what to do, she said.

Oh, Doro trusted her feelings, she would feel it when he stopped loving her whether his clothes smelled of stale smoke or not. He did still love her just as he always had done. At times, however, he surprised himself, even if Doro didn't; he was sometimes oppressed by guilt in the afternoon, in broad daylight, although he hadn't done anything to be ashamed of. Luckily such feelings became much less distinct at dusk, dissipating entirely once night fell and he took his hat and went out again.

So it could probably have gone on for years. Then Dana suddenly disappeared. Apparently because a considerable sum of money had gone missing from the till when the drinks bought were reckoned up against the takings. Paulus had obviously only just checked the figures, promptly blaming his waitress for the discrepancy. Although of course she protested her innocence. Her, innocent? Paulus asked across the bar as he polished a glass to sparkling radiance, and he was sure of the nods all round. When customers nevertheless threatened to go off and drink wherever Dana turned up to wait if he didn't take her back, he assured them that he'd rather go bust.

Schepp listened calmly to all this, sitting at his usual place beneath the wooden vault and working his way, sip by sip, towards a decision. It was no good, you had to bow to the unrelenting nature of existence, you had to reconcile yourself to whatever happened and would happen, you had to accept your fate or be dashed to pieces against it – this, or something like it, is how Schepp was thinking as he picked his way through the situation. And thought that if it turned out badly for him, at least he'd know the right place to attack, indeed to bite.

Shortly thereafter Schepp observed himself speaking casually to Paulus, bringing the conversation around to Dana and her 'misappropriation' of funds, striking his forehead and confiding that now, embarrassingly, it was clear that the whole thing probably should be chalked up to his account, literally so. It was not the real Schepp, of course, who confessed to Paulus, making a very obvious effort to be discreet, that all those weeks and months he had let Dana chalk up what he owed. The missing sum could only be the amount she had secretly cancelled on his behalf. Paulus tugged awkwardly at his moustache, not sure what to think of this story, then decided not to complicate matters even further and unnecessarily, and named a sum he thought appropriate. Schepp was alarmed by the amount but did not hesitate for a moment; yes, it must be something like that, could he settle up with his credit card?

Which made Dana's innocence clear and gave Paulus no option but to apologize to her immediately and ask her to come back and work for him, after all, he wasn't a monster – in fact, Schepp ought to give her the glad news himself, he said, handing him the telephone that stood on the bar. He was sure the Professor could explain it to her better.

Schepp had enough presence of mind to put this off until the following day. He didn't like to call anyone so late, he said, perhaps Paulus would be kind enough to write the number down? Paulus stroked his moustache even more thoroughly than usual, but then he even wrote down the Polish country code. Yes, a call to her would cost money, what had Schepp been thinking?

Schepp preferred to leave that question open. A few days later Dana was back serving drinks at La Pfiff as if she had never been away, and she thanked him by observing him very carefully from the bar, so carefully that it wasn't quite seemly, and then she brought him his wine, ostentatiously breathing in an undertone, 'I dreamt of you again last night.' Schepp was accustomed to mockery of that kind from her, it meant nothing at all, it was just what he expected.

It did, however, surprise him that she never once took a smoking break. Only when nearly everyone had left, and she still hadn't said or done anything that she didn't say or do at every other table, did Schepp give himself a push and go over to the bar to pay; he almost stumbled, the wine affected his legs so suddenly. As she printed out the receipt Dana turned to him in such a way that the tattoo was right in his face. Sorting the notes she asked how she could ever repay him for 'all that', but her eyes did not sparkle as she spoke. It was on the tip of Schepp's tongue to say, oh, it will be enough if some day I can give that damn throat of yours a good bite, but immediately a rushing began in his ears, his jaw worked idly, and he said nothing. Or did he? He must have said something or other in his confusion; with that rushing in your ears you couldn't hear yourself speak. Dana suddenly laughed so indignantly that the rushing stopped at once, and everyone still sitting with their glasses looked up..

Schepp remembered only those glances directed at him, an overexposed snapshot in his memory that faded everything else out, a still moment of terror into which, powerfully, eternity had passed. Then the picture started moving again. Dana turned away from him with contempt and began, with a 'That takes even *my* breath away!', to pull him to pieces. In so far as he could hear at all, what with the rushing in his ears, that terrible rushing. He didn't know whether to feel offended as a man or as someone who had, after all, shelled out a considerable sum of money for Dana and now had to listen to her putting him down in the most brazen way.

Today, when he reconstructed the scene, he felt sick with embarrassment; he would have liked to have kept his eyes firmly shut until it was entirely forgotten. He ought really to have told Doro about it long ago, but the story had not point – apart perhaps from the fact that he had never felt so ashamed in his life, what was there to say? Soon after he had unselfishly paid off Dana's debts, she had disappeared again anyway. This time for good. Paulus didn't know why. No, she had left of her own accord, disappeared from one day to the next, that was her way, he had no means of keeping her.

And this time Schepp had no means of getting her back. Yes, he kept ringing her at different times of the day and night, but he always got her voicemail, left good wishes 'from all at La Pfiff', at first even whistled a little goodbye tune. His sense of humour took a beating when, one day, the digital voice told him that the number he wanted was unavailable – Schepp understood at once, even if he didn't get a word of the Polish message. He cursed the doctor who had advised him to have his eye operation. In his old half-blind condition he would never have found his way to La Pfiff, would never have seen Dana and therefore would not be missing her now, missing her in this pathetic way. If only he had stayed in the peaceful routine of his old life with his wonderful wife! Who now lay dead beside him, and had taken any resentment she might have had with her –

Taken it with her?

On the contrary. Schepp flew into a rage. Behind his back, she had maliciously compiled a reckoning, had left him all her resentment in black and white, and he couldn't even contradict it. Oh no? He'd see if he couldn't! Once again he was pacing back and forth in full flow, one last time, right hand keeping precise time in the air with his thoughts, index and little fingers, the rest of his hand a clenched fist.

He was so angry with Doro (even though he had been angry with the ophthalmologist a moment earlier) that he could have knocked her down or done something else to hurt her.

Schepp stamped, Schepp snorted, Schepp was a caged wild beast, he was going to bite the next hand that came close, watch out! When the doorbell rang he stood still for a moment, holding his breath, but it would only be the postman looking for the nearest idiot to deliver some neighbour's package to. The hell with the postman. The doorbell rang a second time, rang in a demanding way and for rather too long. Schepp stood there trembling, gasping for breath, his glance roaming until it came to rest on Doro's nose. The nose definitely looked sharper, he didn't need convincing, her face was altogether thinner.

Bonier.

Uglier.

Yes, he hissed, you've become uglier. Your own fault. It serves you right.

From outside came the sound of a car driving away, from inside not even a buzzing, even the fly was hiding from him. A few breaths later he discovered it crawling out of Doro's nose. 'Filthy creature!' he shouted, so loudly that it immediately settled on Doro's cheek. The way it crawled out and the way it settled struck him as outrageous, incredibly nasty. All the bottled-up anger against

Doro tried to discharge itself in determined gesticulating: 'You just wait, you'll be sorry!'

The fly showed no alarm at his flapping. 'Damn you, get out!' If it stayed on Doro's cheek he surely couldn't – ? Then it all suddenly poured out of him. A desperate bitterness about his entire life: about the Emperor of China, whom as a little boy he had been so keen to meet and who had enticed him into this wretched life as a Sinologist; about his colleagues who had laughed at him for years; about his mother who had always blamed him for being a failure because he hadn't become a professor, as if he hadn't done far, far more in life than she had – she who hadn't even been able to provide him with a proper father; about his parents-in-law, who thought that their daughter should have married someone better, and who had insisted on a prenuptial agreement with a strict division of property; about Doro, who never openly contradicted them to declare her belief in him, who had in fact withdrawn more and more as the years went on, as if they were living together only for the sake of their children – what was left of the dream they had shared, the one in which she dreamt about a lake with or without an isle of the dead in it? About Pia, who had fled as far as possible from her parental home as soon as she had her school-leaving certificate, as if she'd been any happier in the United States, as if she could ever have made it there, with her poor linguistic ability; about Louisa, who had meant everything to him but since puberty had fallen so short of all he had hoped she would be; about his doctoral students with their pathetically mediocre minds; about the ophthalmologist; about La Pfiff and every single person waiting for someone, looking for something; about Dana, who had come so unexpectedly into his life and disappeared from it equally unexpectedly. Who did she think she was, what right did she have to go through life so high-handedly, bringing nothing but confusion with her, wreaking havoc, leaving emptiness in her wake? A dark, gloomy storm was brewing inside Schepp, all the gloom he had kept within bounds all his life through persistent study of the ancient sources. Since his operation, following the trail of all things bright and colourful, it had crawled back into his life and devoured it.

The fly took off into the air.

Schepp followed in hot pursuit. It must atone for its sins. Ignoring in his fury the vase of flowers as it fell over and broke behind him, he struck out at the fly with the manuscript, now wielding the stack of paper with both fists, now rolling it up in his right hand. A few sheets came loose and fluttered to the floor. Schepp took no notice, he was focused on his rage. Wherever the fly came down he was after it like doom personified. Who cared if an object fell off the desk or the coffee table, fell off the shelf and rolled across the floor, even breaking?

Then, head bent over, arms hanging powerless by his sides, he just sat there. On the ceiling, equally motionless, sat the fly. When the clock of the Church of the Good Shepherd struck first four high notes and then three low notes, Schepp knew what time it had struck, but didn't know how the tears were pouring down his cheeks.

Finally he drew up his knees and buried his face in his hands, hoping for a miracle. If it hadn't been for that smell! Schepp could discern it more and more clearly, that indecent something Other that had been waiting to ambush him this morning at the heart of his familiar home, that had maliciously skewed the day. How could flower water stink like that? Although when he knelt in front of the puddle that had spread among the broken pieces, the water smelt of nothing at all.

Not in the least?

Not in the least. Schepp inhaled. Such an intolerably unique smell had never entered his nostrils before. Should he fling all the windows open, should he get rid of everything in the room that was quietly, eerily, giving off that smell, trying to drive him mad? It couldn't be Doro, thank God; he remembered her perfume, a bottle of it had stood on the desk ever since their wedding so that he always had the scent of her nearby when he surfaced from his texts and wanted to be reassured of her love. When had he last seen the little bottle of perfume? He hoped the fluid in it hadn't evaporated.

He found the flask intact, removed the stopper, closed his eyes, and for a few seconds he could imagine that everything was all right, was as it had been thirty years before. He dabbed some of the perfume behind Doro's ears and at the base of her throat. There, that was better. He checked that her hands remained as he had folded them. By now they were considerably more rigid. Linked inseparably, they somewhat resembled claws. As he smoothed the sleeve of the kimono he saw more discoloured patches on her body and carefully covered them up again. Yes, that was better.

Now he'd get it over and done with. Quietly, Schepp went around the room, carefully avoiding anything in his path, retrieving the sheets of his manuscript that he still had to read. There were not many, barely three pages. Doro's final set of comments began on the third page. He could cope with her comments now too. He put all the pages in the correct order. And then? He would be done. And afterwards for all he cared the doctor could come, the undertaker, the lawyer to read the will, the executor. He sat down beside Doro on the *chaise-longue*. When he located the passage in which Marek was asked for his name and date of birth at the customs office, and was taken into custody, his own name was still there in the margin. 'Why not just call him Hinrich and be done with it?' At that point Schepp would have liked to stop reading again. But it was no good. He had promised.

After they'd taken away his belt and his boots they gave him a cell that was, roughly speaking, three times the size of the mattress in his Dolly, the barred window hardly as big as the new skylight. But why, what was going on? Although they didn't know, they did tell him, shrugging, that matters would take their course, was there anyone he wanted to phone? Then Marek, without stopping to think, put his hand in the breast pocket of his jacket and found only the note with Hanni's phone number. That wasn't going to be any help. Hanni! Come to think of it, hadn't she got him into this shitty situation in the first place? If she hadn't said that one thing to him, he'd never have driven off. In winter! With summer tyres on the van. All because of a woman who probably didn't think much of men anyway, and he, Marek, had been made a laughing stock by such a person. He was bloody furious!

Big Marek. They gave him some time to calm down. Twice he rang for the customs man who had arrested him and who assured him that everything would be all right, the investigating judge had been informed. Finally, after four hours, things started moving, as we found out later, much later, when we heard the entire story, all the details: he was carted all over the place, ended up in the office of the investigating judge, who had apparently just been on the phone to the judge responsible for such matters in Marek's hometown. And she, the judge in his hometown, had told this judge that the reason for his arrest was an unpaid parking fine, because he had once left the Dolly in a no-parking zone. The reminder had been sent to his parents' address, which was still Marek's official place of residence. The letter had probably simply disappeared in a pile of their other post, ditto the summons to turn up in court.

Marek was no longer a potential enemy of the state or serious offender, he was just a little fish again. After surrendering his savings passbook as bail, he was allowed to leave on the condition that he report to the judge in his hometown within twenty-four hours. That meant ... but when he was taken back to the customs office, the officers there had been spending their time checking his Dolly van, and had found a whole list of things that, in their view, made it un-roadworthy. The most serious was the little skylight, not mentioned in the vehicle documents and therefore not passed by the MOT office. They were sorry but the registration of his Dolly van was invalid, he couldn't continue his journey, and he had to pay a fine of sixty marks.

Marek burst into tears. They'd finally got their claws into him.

But hadn't he been told, by a higher authority, that he had to turn up back home within twenty-four hours, so surely he *must* be allowed to leave? The very same customs man who arrested him in the first place now persuades his superior to reinstate Marek's right to drive the van home. So they tell him to take his old heap of scrap metal to the local MOT office within the next twenty-four hours, and when they hear about his savings passbook they even tear up the sixty-mark fine.

Marek races on like a world champion. First in driving snow, taking as a guide the space where the central reservation might be; then in heavy rain, water coming in not only through the holes in the van's floor but also from above; they probably bent the fitting of the skylight out of true during their inspection. When he finally crosses the finishing line here, well after midnight, he goes straight to the Blaue Maus. A notice on the door instantly makes him suspicious. He goes closer, flicking his lighter to read it. 'Mutt has passed away. Closed for the funeral.'

Marek half-heartedly rattles the door, he isn't to know, and in this situation he certainly wouldn't want to know, that by this time Wolfi has closed down entirely and gone to manage some bar or other in Bavaria, while the notice has been scribbled over quite a lot, so he could have worked out for himself that Mutt must have been dead for some time. Never mind! Marek needs someone he can talk to about his journey, someone who might even console him, and he also needs a place to spend the night that won't seem as miserable and lonely as his Dolly. He puts his hand in his jacket pocket and finds the piece of paper with Hanni's phone number, which indeed could come in really handy right about now; after all, she still owes him a night. In fact as soon as he finds a phone kiosk and lets the phone ring on at her place until she answers, she says, 'Sure,' or 'Okay,' or 'Are you crazy?' – we don't know for certain, but anyway he drives over there.

When she opens the door to him there are no little gold flecks sparkling in her brown eyes. Far from it, she stares at him like he was some kind of apparition. Marek, however, stammers it all out, confused as he is, what with the rushing in his ears he can hardly hear himself speak. In retrospect all he can remember is that maybe he asked her if she really didn't fancy men? Only dykes? Imagine that! Anyway, Hanni looks at him so incredulously, and a second later starts laughing so indignantly, that the rushing in his ears stops for a moment, and

And then what? Then nothing. The text broke off; that was where he had stopped writing. He sat there dumbstruck. In the margin Doro had written, 'As if he'd have said anything like that in such a situation. Don't kid yourself, that's not the end of the story.' She had continued writing where he had stopped, or, to be more accurate, she had begun rewriting the scene between the lines a few paragraphs earlier. Rewritten it in such a way that it was soon very like the one in which Dana, after her misappropriation of the cash or whatever you want to call it, came back to wait tables at La Pfiff and was as indifferent, yes, indifferent to Schepp as if she had never been sacked without notice and then got her job back only because he lied gallantly on her behalf. Not a single detail remained of the midnight encounter between Marek and Hanni. The end of the story now read:

Only when Schepp had stood up and gone to the bar to pay did she ask him how she could ever repay him for 'all that'. There was none of the usual sparkle in her look, though, even on a day like that one where there should have been. In his confusion Schepp droned on, barely able to hear himself speak for the rushing in his ears. In retrospect all he thought he could remember was that he had condescendingly given her to understand that 'a woman like her' could presumably only 'pay in kind, and in instalments' for what he had spent to get her out of trouble. Dana looked at him so incredulously, and a second later laughed so indignantly, that the rushing in his ears stopped for a moment and everyone looked up.

'Well, better begin right away, then!' she cried, grabbing him with both hands, bending him back over the bar and leaning over him.

Not to kiss him – 'Does that old fool seriously think …?' – but to spit in his face. When she finally let go of him she was baring her teeth. Schepp struggled up, breathing heavily, and wiped his face with the handkerchief from his breast pocket. A mistake! he would have liked to assure her, a bad joke! Good God, hadn't he had to put up with many of her own bad jokes? While he was still gasping for air, Dana was already turning away, ripping him to shreds at the top of her voice in front of the remaining customers. It wasn't long before one of them, a young fellow known as Kiddo, staggered over to the Professor and gave *him* a lecture, if you could call it that, because Kiddo was so sozzled he could hardly utter a coherent sentence.

There could be a saint even inside a waitress, that was the gist of it; did that old jerk think he could pester her with his improper advances, did he really think he could fumble her with his grubby paws?

Normally Schepp would have calmed everyone down quickly with a few rhetorical flourishes, but the young fellow took him by the lapels and pulled him close, bad breath wafting in his face. Someone like him, said Kiddo, needed a good thrashing, he'd earned it, but – and here he pushed Schepp away so that he hit the bar, waiting speechless for what came next – but a man like the Professor wasn't worth a straight right or left, man to man, he wasn't even a quarter of a man, so a slap in the face – and here Kiddo gave him a resounding one – would have to do for now. Schepp exited the building.

And hardly dared to breathe. While reading, his remaining powers of resistance had been extinguished, for – for what Doro had written was strikingly like what had actually happened, practically verbatim, there was no point in denying it. He couldn't even fool himself any more. Confronted so unexpectedly with the wretched details of that night, he saw the whole scene in his mind's eye, an intolerably well-lit image surfacing from his memory, an image in which the glances the others shot his way paled in insignificance. As if it hadn't happened five years ago but just yesterday. He had gone home like a beaten dog swearing never, ever to set foot in La Pfiff again. He could have died of shame; he had wanted only to forget it, keep it secret, suppress it until it had vanished from his memory, until no one knew about it any more, until it had never happened. But Doro, whom he most particularly would not have told about it, appeared very well informed, knew every detail, even knew about that embarrassing request to be paid 'in kind'.

Schepp put down the sheet of paper. There was no glossing it over any more. His past faux pas, or rather his offence, or rather the stain on his life, was there in his file in black and white. Doro had deprived him of any opportunity to fashion an alibi through rhetorical manipulation of the facts. He was as deeply ashamed as he had been on that night five years ago, not least of being described as someone not even worth a straight punch, a right or left between equals. Doro had even known about that – and had never said a word.

There were a few more pages which she used for editorial notes. He had not expected much from those, but now he knew that they would go to the heart of the matter.

Yet he had so often sat in judgement on himself, oh how he had regretted it, how he had resolved to return to his old life, seeking happiness in the old heroic tales, the brushstrokes of ancient Chinese calligraphy. But happiness was no longer to be found there. He had thrown out the coloured handkerchiefs he'd worn in his breast pocket, he had let his hair grow out and combed it over his bald patch the way he used to. But beneath the surface his thoughts had simply run on. Had he at least begun to avoid La Pfiff, had he chosen to drink in some other bar? No. Perhaps the worst thing was that in spite of his double humiliation – as if Dana's hadn't been enough, as if he'd needed another from a young man like Kiddo to open his eyes – he couldn't bring himself to draw a line under the whole business, that after two or three weeks without being able to whistle his usual goodbye to Dana, he couldn't stand it any longer. Acting as naturally as possible, he had turned up at La Pfiff again.

But no one took any notice – because hardly any of the old late-night regulars were still there. The dreary atmosphere of former days was back again. No one minded who came there now, not even if it was Schepp. And this time Paulus didn't know why Dana had disappeared. Or where she'd gone. Maybe back to Poland, he conjectured; anyhow it was better that way. For the Professor too, he added, stroking his moustache.

Better that way, yes, certainly. Although of course it was the worst thing of all, it was unbearable. To see Schepp return to his regular table, order his red wine, spend the evenings in silent dialogue, sometimes allowing himself to scan the place as if looking for something in particular – well, no one would have taken him for a renowned international expert in anything. And Doro, whom he had always loved faithfully, stayed the same even in these difficult years. With her natural elegance of mind, she rose quietly above his ingrained melancholy. He was so lonely when they were together, she might have understood that from his clumsy grin, a grin that really meant to be a smile, most really of all an exclamation mark. But at most Doro cocked her head at him and said nothing. Hadn't she become even a bit cooler, more distant, more reserved, as if, in her intuitively vegetative way, she had picked up on his dismal failure and wanted to avoid it for herself? Was she secretly ashamed for him, was she suffering with him so much that she was hiding her empathy?

Discontented, Schepp regarded the gloomy sketch of his life, remembering how he had hardly been able to write a line, how in desperation he had looked for old essays and papers that might be worth revising, how he had finally come upon *Marek the Drunkard*. He remembered staring at the typescript and suddenly recalling the scene he had meant to write decades before, the scene where Marek had to report to the police first thing the next morning and then go to the MOT office. Where after a brief inspection of load-bearing parts he was told that he could count himself lucky to be getting off without a hefty fine, but in any case it would be without his Dolly. No, he would not be allowed to drive it so much as a metre away from the MOT testing station, it was hereby withdrawn from circulation and sent for scrap. There stood Marek with a bag of possessions hurriedly salvaged from his home; he would have liked to have shrugged, but instead the tears were pouring down his cheeks. He had no home any more, there was nothing for it, he'd have to call Hanni and ask if she might additionally allow him a day. But Schepp hadn't even tried to write this little scene. The manuscript, unread, had soon disappeared under a stack of papers in a cupboard or drawer. And so, somehow, things had gone on and on, day after day. He managed to continue teaching; as for his research, he had stopped nurturing any ambitions in that department long since. His eye fell on the cap of the fountain pen lying under the coffee table, much too far away for him to retrieve it. He didn't hear the clock of the Church of the Good Shepherd strike four high notes and then four low notes, he didn't feel another tear run down his cheek. He picked up his manuscript with both hands – what else was there for him to hold on to? – and read what Doro had written at the end of the story.

No, Hinrich, I know very well that even that can't be the end. It's taken me a few years to summon up the courage to think as much and, more to the point, to tell you so. I'm relieved now, even if I find it a little embarrassing, that I had to make use of your old story. Yes, Hinrich, I know you're not Marek and definitely not Jörn. I'm sure you only worshipped this Hanni from afar, hidden among your friends at the other end of the bar. At the time I probably loved you, my little would-be Marek, more than you ever let yourself dream I might. Did you maybe stay a would-be Marek until your eye operation? Anyway, you were certainly not a man who could make a woman feel secure for an entire lifetime.

I'll cheerfully admit to doing violence to that old text of yours; it's been a while since you used a typewriter. I'll also confess that at no time was I concerned with correcting your story in any detail – whether misappropriation of cash or destruction of bar fittings was the point at issue, whether it was Jörn or Kiddo or Wolfi or Paul, what difference does it make? I have been speechless in our marriage, and here I finally saw my chance to tell you how hard the last five years have been for me, maybe even the last twenty-five years. Forgive me, I lacked the courage to try to discuss it with you. It seems to me that we were never able to find a means of communication that would have brought us together in anything other than a mundane way. There were the texts you had written and that I edited. Presumably you wouldn't have paid attention to anything but a written text. If I know you, you wouldn't understand anything but editorial corrections.

Understand what?

Oh, a great deal, Hinrich.

Firstly: It was a mere single sentence in this little text of yours that caught my eye, a naïve audacious remark you repeated thirty years later in the face of another woman. A shockingly wrong thing said at the wrong time, the kind of thing only men can utter. The first time you probably only thought it or heard it somewhere, but then you actually said it – you dared to say it to a woman like Dana, say it to her face. How angry she was with you! So was I. How could I have been married for twenty-nine years to someone who would so much as venture to think up that remark? What had happened to the shy dreamer of the old days, who had held a woman's hand for the first time at the age of thirty-five? But then you held it so tightly that I might well have thought it meant a good deal. You became a would-be Marek, or a would-be man instead of a would-be Marek.

Please forgive me, it is not, of course, just that remark that has made me so angry. It's the pathetic lover-boy who expresses all his small-minded pathos in it. You're a jumped-up nobody, you have no discretion, no decency, no tact, you have no sensitivity at all even in adultery. And you're also a failure, Hinrich; oddly enough that hurts me too. Didn't you buy Dana, at least according to your shabby logic? Wouldn't you have thrown her down that very same night – you, with her! –

on the bar or somewhere else, telling her she *had* taken money from the till, so that as you saw it she owed you? Shouldn't it therefore have been repaid, every penny of it, 'in kind' – my God, have you any idea how that sounds to a woman? And how has it in fact been repaid? I'm sorry, Hinrich, I am not thinking about morality, I am thinking about style. You're all the same, men and would-be men, and, to be absolutely clear, I despise you more than ever.

No, what I wrote yesterday isn't true; I don't despise you, you have been punished enough. I am ashamed of you, Hinrich, and I share a little of that shame myself. At the time, anyway, when Dana told me how she had to bring you to your senses, I could have cursed you. If I hadn't already been cursing you for your nocturnal escapades, your ever-changing affairs, maybe I would have wanted the ground to swallow me up there in front of her. Imagine having a strange woman tell you all that about your own husband.

Yet I wasn't as surprised as you might think. Did you suppose I wouldn't notice anything? Yes, while you were still groping your way through life half blind, I was good enough for you. While I was editing what you wrote, you were happy to assure me that you would even hold my hand in the next world. But as soon as you could see properly, whose hand did you hold? You owe me an explanation, Hinrich. Do you seriously think I never noticed how much you had changed? How you turned away from what had meant everything to you before? And, let me say in passing, what it meant to me. Did you think I would just sit back and let it happen, when I had wanted to be happy with you for ever? I gave you my word in front of witnesses, could you forget that?

Yes, you could. You left me. Not physically, I know, but in every other way. Because I am now, at last, also leaving you, I will call you Schepp again, so that you understand I take this seriously, I really have drawn a line underneath it. The Hinrich I knew and loved, and with whom I hoped to grow old, disappeared from my life after his eye operation. Only the pathetic remains are left. Yes, Schepp, you read that correctly, and because I am leaving you I want to have it out in the clear light of day and

At this point Schepp was overwhelmed by helpless, hysterical laughter, which gave him a fright. He then stared into space for a while, finally blew his nose and said, a distinct note of doubt in his voice, 'Then this really is a farewell letter? She surely won't have done herself, well, an injury – done anything silly?'

No, Schepp had no tears left; all he could do was read on, and there were only about a dozen pages left. He had good reason to wonder what that woman Dana had said about him; he knew she could be economical with the truth. Oh, how could Doro be so credulous, how could she believe what a woman like Dana said? Now that she didn't even want to call him by his first name, did he have to call her Fräulein Dorothee again, maybe even Fräulein von Hagelstein? He glanced at the parquet beneath the slanting rays of the afternoon sun, where remnants of his life lay scattered. Now, in the softer light, he could make out details of the photographs without squinting. There could easily have been some memory or other among them, he could have dived down, submerged himself instead of giving himself over to what he still had to read. But he did not. He plucked up his courage and did not stop again.

Yes, Schepp, what you have read is correct; because I am leaving you, I want to have it out in the clear light of day and confess something to you. I too have been unfaithful, for at least as long as you and with far greater consistency. Not the way you are imagining. Although of course I was crazy about her, used every opportunity to meet up with her – at least I can understand you there. How strong she was, bubbling over with *joie de vivre*, the life force. When I saw her the first time, leaning against the bar, I knew instantly what drove you there evening after evening. After all, I'd felt for weeks that you had changed completely, I sensed it after that night you came home so late, not really of this world, or at least not entirely responsible for your actions.

You could be forgiven for that, I know that now. But asking to borrow my commentaries on the I Ching the very next day, keeping the book for weeks on end – the I Ching, of all things, the text you usually refer to with mild derision, don't you think that was a bit tasteless? Or did you really think me so simple-minded? Did you actually not care? Unloved wives are jealous. You underestimate a placid surface; it masks hidden depths. The quieter I became, the more violent I felt inside. And I'm not supposed to get upset. But high blood pressure doesn't count for much when you're coming to terms with your husband's baser instincts.

Once you start seeking, you find. Even if at first all you find is a short yellowed typescript – why did you never tell me that you'd tried your hand at a novel? Or was it just going to be a short story? At any rate, you went at it, shall we say, full tilt in a way I'd never have expected you to. Forgive me, but did you really write it yourself? You weren't the kind of man who stood at the bar, you were much more of an outsider, like Marek – were you trying to write about yourself? Well, you weren't nearly as unworldly as I thought you were before your operation. If I'd guessed … would I have fallen in love with such a Schepp?

But back to Dana. The way you kept looking at her while you were talking on the phone to Pia! You clearly cared so little about our daughter's divorce that I immediately drew my own conclusions. It probably escaped your notice, in fact of course it escaped your notice, that I made a date that very evening to meet up with Dana. As soon as I saw that sign tattooed on her throat, everything was clear; I was electrified: *Kan*, the double water sign, I'd meditated on it for years, it couldn't be a coincidence. I had to approach her. And so I did. Dana had wanted to be approached, as I now know. Or do you think she met up with anyone and everyone just for fun? Not that she didn't enjoy it, she certainly wouldn't have done anything that she didn't want to do. But she made sure she got paid. I pretended I merely wanted to pass the time while you were on the phone to Pia, said something along the lines of, 'Do you know what you actually got stuck with there?'

Dana thought I was cracking a joke and rolled her eyes. 'A helluva lot of men.'

'A helluva lot of water, as it happens.' Did she want to know more?

'That's a new one on me!' Yes, she said, she was extremely interested, she loved water, she'd always been a good swimmer.

She pretended she thought the sign was just some kind of modern graphic art. But when, probably inspired by the *Kan* sign itself, I said I could tell her more about the meaning of her Chinese character, she agreed at once. I found out later that you had approached her in the same way. Do you in fact have any idea what *Kan* means? I didn't fail to notice that you were collecting information from my commentaries, you even underlined the relevant passages. But one doesn't come to understand the I Ching within a few days. For that to happen you have to make a serious study of it. You may not believe me, but in secretly making a first date with Dana, naïve as I was, all I wanted was to protect you from her. She would have robbed you blind, I thought, she would have ruined you, a man like you would have been right up her street – if at the last minute you didn't do something so foolish that it would hurt her pride. You underestimated her pride. Otherwise, who knows, she might not have remained so aloof.

When I found out that there was not, as I'd originally assumed, an affectionate understanding between the two of you, I immediately decided to prevent one from forming. Admittedly, even then I was not uninterested in Dana myself. Be that as it may, I wanted there to be something between her and me, something stronger than you could imagine in your besotted intriguing – do you understand? I got in before you did. I seduced her. Oh no, not in the way you're thinking with your pathetically one-sided imagination. But no less tenaciously and, above all, far more consistently.

At first I was a somewhat unexpected confidante to whom Dana could tell everything about you that I didn't want to know. She scornfully enumerated all your earlier affairs and would-be affairs. I don't have to tell you about those, I'm sure. It's amazing what she knew about you. She told me in detail how you pursued her from the first moment, with looks, with insinuating remarks. Soon even intruding on her smoking breaks, when she really would have liked to be on her own. You deserved to be rejected unreservedly. But I wanted to be sure, so on the day after you received that slap in the face I went from being her confidante to being her accomplice – we'd been meeting up regularly for a long time, exchanging information about you – and got her a new mobile and phone contract. Yes, you have me to thank for being eventually unable to reach her on that number. You're surprised, I'm sure; you wouldn't have thought it of me, would you? I often listened to your messages on the old mobile later, when my determination began to waver. Do I have to repeat what you cooed and whistled to her? Astonishing to think what an amorous fool is hidden inside even you. I'd never have suspected you of such folly.

Back to Dana. At first I didn't take any real interest in her, apart from her tattoo. We found her a job at another bar a few streets away, where she could wait tables again until one of the men chasing her would turn too insistent. That should have been the moment for me to say goodbye to her. But by then I could no longer do it. I wanted to win her for myself. Isn't she a fascinating person? You'd be the last to contradict me. Isn't she, how shall I put it, isn't she a woman through and through?

No, it's not how you think it is. She didn't have half as many affairs as you assume, in fact not a single one; after all, she had other worries. A family to feed, mother, grandmother, child – you'd never have dreamt that she's a mother, would you? Her little boy is growing up in the same farmhouse where she grew up instead of at home with her parents. The fields have been sold off, it seems that nothing is left from the old days except the misery. 'Either it was raining or the gate at the level crossing was closed,' that's how Dana summed it up. She'd already done 'everything she could' to make sure her family could manage, everything – do you know what that means? I'd rather not imagine it in any detail. Without sometimes fleecing one or another of the men pursuing her tenaciously, without going off with some of the takings now and then, she couldn't have coped. And then that curse that seemed to pursue her, always driving her on. Fundamentally she was always fleeing. How else could she escape from the importunate world?

You know what I mean. You're condemned to know. In spite of everything, she was very much at ease in her own body; maybe that was what I most admired – she was so incurably healthy. While making herself out to be impulsive, confused, unpredictable, she was clear-minded and realistic and focused about what she wanted – and she almost always got it.

Is it surprising that things turned out as they were bound to? At only our second meeting she asked me, mockingly, whether my lover did the housework while I was out – not my husband, you will notice. How do you like that? It surely *must* be confusing, don't you think? Once, you will hardly believe me, she bid me goodbye with the words, 'Tonight I shall dream of you again.' Admit it, that wouldn't have left you cold either. Then it all happened very quickly, but not the way you're thinking. Much worse: it became a real friendship.

Or perhaps not entirely a real friendship.

It's difficult for me to write about it. Put into words, it would all suddenly seem so trivial, so ordinary, yet it really was something special.

I have paused for a while in writing this letter; I still have three days, three mornings when I can sit here and finish it. Almost like old times. As far as Dana and I are concerned, I will spare you the details; we met up as often as circumstances allowed, and that was often. I would not say that I kept her financially, like all the others before me; our relationship was fundamentally different from the one you dreamt of. Besides, we are reasonably well off and secure ourselves, a little money more or less makes no difference. Hadn't she endured the shipwreck of her life? Wasn't she doomed to be shipwrecked again and again? Was it not *incumbent* upon me to help her whenever I could, if only out of simple humanity?

I have paused again in my writing. Dr Regelsberger says I should not – get so het up. Yes, my relationship with Dana soon became – how shall I put it? – soon became very close. Not that you should think I had no pangs of conscience; I did. But wasn't it you who started it? Should it not, consequently, have been up to you to put an end to it, or at least try to, you whom I have always loved faithfully? But even during those emotional times you didn't change, following your gloomy course without sparing a thought for me. I felt so lonely when we were together! You should have realized that I desperately wanted to talk to you, if only because I avoided it so persistently. Instead you let your hair grow out again, as if that would change something inside your head. When we drank our tea in the afternoon you went back to stroking it over your bald patch just as you had done before. Yet nothing was the same. Nothing.

Isn't it outrageous, positively detestable, that you never noticed that anything was wrong? How could you be so indifferent to me? But you only ever loved me as you might love a perfect flower arrangement, a beautiful accessory, an arabesque in the margin of your life. For years I tried to reconcile myself to that, to adjust to it. After your operation it was harder and harder for me, and then overnight it actually became impossible. Our time together had run out.

Did you know that her name is really Danuta? I always called her Danka, which she liked. I think it was what she had been called as a child. No, I never told her about my dark thoughts, simply because when I was with her they did not exist. She was so lively that there was no space left for the melancholy that has afflicted me all my life. Within the first few weeks she did what you have been unable to do for thirty years – you have no idea how I can laugh. As if her mere presence released me, relieved me of the burden I have always carried. All that had made my days so quiet and hard to bear had turned to air.

Then came the moment when she disappeared from my life too. Not entirely without trace, as she disappeared from yours. Tomorrow will be the first anniversary of her farewell, and I look forward to the day with great joy. At the time, however, although I had always expected it to happen, I was rather distressed, and I was still distressed weeks later. You never noticed; I had already kept my illnesses from you: the neurologist's diagnosis, the results of the CT scan. For you, after all, I was always to be the woman you married twenty-nine years ago, anything else would just have been a nuisance. So now, as the old Doro, I will say goodbye.

Well, Dana left me too, just as she has left everyone. So in the end you and I have something in common again, Schepp, who would have thought it possible? But while you have only one evening to remember for the rest of your life, I have four years. Four wonderful years. She had to move on, who knows why, the confused circumstances of her life were never entirely clear even to me. I had only just lent her a little money, but that can't have been the reason; I did not even mention it when we parted. The only explanation she gave was that it was never too late to make the right decision, she had to go back to where she came from, it was high time she did.

I asked no further questions. You know that wasn't the way to get anything out of her. She was planning to leave in a few days anyway, her decision had been made. What a look she gave me when we parted, so full of the tender affection that is possible only between women. Not in the way you may think, but – more comprehensive, more final. A look that I shall never forget.

It was nearly a year before I could bring myself to make my decision. After all, we have a family, an apartment, destinies to be disentangled. Above all, I had, and have, a conscience! How quickly the two of us, you and I, have grown apart. It began when we stopped sharing a bedroom, and went on from there. But how well we managed, all the same, no upsetting scenes, no major discord, almost perfect – if it hadn't been for Dana it would have gone on until death did us part. Now life is parting us, and I feel ashamed not where you're concerned but for myself. I did not *want* to write to tell you that I am leaving you – I have always thought of marriage as a sacred bond. Only Dana's farewell look gave me the strength to do it.

Just as I was the one who took her away from you, now she is taking me away from you. Yes, our ways part tomorrow, Schepp. What would we humans be without the freedom to set out somewhere whenever we want, anywhere, against all reason? At least I have a path to follow, at least I can say that I shall be going to a place where I may perhaps really arrive. Or where I belong. You know, heavy hearts sink faster, and I want mine to be light again, at least as light as it was when we first met. If everything that happens to us is really only an echo of what we carry inside us, then in the end that path will lead me to where I can discover my innermost, deepest, most hidden being, all that I have forbidden myself in past years.

So much for my confession. I am under some pressure because I must finish my farewell letter tomorrow. When you come into this room, I expect around eleven, I shall already be on my way. Around two or half past someone will call to take away what I have packed over the last few days. Please be sensible and do not cause any unnecessary difficulties. For the moment, anyway, I am taking only the bare essentials. You don't have to worry about telling Pia and Louisa; they already know. Of course in the next few days you will be hearing from my lawyer – no half measures any more, what must be must be. I assure you that he will soon come to an agreement with you. At least, it has all been discussed and prepared, with the requisite powers of attorney.

Do you think me cruel? It is only logical. What you did to me all these years was cruel, as was, even more so, what you did not do. But I never complained; if you will be kind enough to look back, you will realize that I was always at your side. Or at least you lacked for nothing. You will keep the books, the texts, the source materials. You will go on living in the same way as before. At worst, you will have to look for some other, shall we say, female companion to drink tea with you in the afternoon. According to Dana you have plenty of choice.

By now I hardly even care. The one thing that still matters to me, as I think for the last time about the two of us, is that I want to have a clear conscience before I leave. The lack of clarity that has come to exist between us over the years is more than I can bear. But how could I have told you, how could I have explained it, when you would have been sure to interrupt me with your constant hair-splitting, or made fun of me in some other way? When I came upon your little story about Marek – for the second time – I finally knew how to clarify matters. What can you do if you no longer have the strength to say something straight out? You find a roundabout way to say it.

It is never too late to begin a new life. I have felt truly euphoric for the past few days. Today the time has come. I have set the date for my departure so that in future I will still have good reason to rejoice on this day. Before I go, it's true, I would like to slap your face, but instead I wish you, with all my heart – what? A long life in which you will have plenty of time to think about these things.

No, that's not true. After all, I did love you, at least until you had your operation. Of course I wish you, with all my heart –

No, that's not it either. From today you are dead to me; don't think I will come back. And after death I won't wait for you either. I will tell you something so that you do not even hope for that. It has to do, and this should not surprise you, with Dana and the sign on her throat. At our first meeting we simply forgot to discuss it, we were busy talking about quite different things, other subjects entirely. Strange, don't you think? Afterwards we never got around to talking about it, although I can hardly believe that in retrospect. Perhaps because there was always so much to laugh about, and the *Kan* character would only have got in the way.

I suppose it must have been as simple as that. Only when we met up one last time to say goodbye did we get around to the sign that had brought us together and that, we were sure, would bring us together again. I told her, and it was high time to do so, what it means, what danger lies within it, and how you can face it by never standing still and staying in one place, by always turning in towards that same danger until you are clear of it, and facing the next one. I don't have to explain to you that *Kan* is a sign that is best – at least according to the Southern Commentaries – left behind as quickly as possible.

Even if one is as magically attracted to it as you or I! That is the teaching of the I Ching: you can never stay with any one of the signs. You must keep abreast of changes so that, within the flow of all beings, you become someone else. You, pursuing your indifferent atheistic train of thought, will never understand this. But even for you, Dana's decision to adorn herself with the sign of the abyss cannot have been pure coincidence. A clear sign of danger, every yang stroke already fallen between its two yin strokes. Most important of all, it consists of water both above and below, water everywhere, a huge lake, almost a sea, I explained to Dana, rather a lot of water for a single lifetime.

'Water, water, water.' Dana's glance was vague – we called it her Galician look. 'I'm usually up to my neck in it, but I'll never drown, I was always a good – '

'I know.' I waved that comment away, she'd often said it before. 'Like a fish in water.' Only then did I realize what had brought us together, and I knew I had to tell her about it, about the cold, dark lake, and how it frightened me.

As soon as I had finished my confession, Dana took my hand. She had an idea, she said – I was so surprised I couldn't protest, let alone withdraw my hand from hers. So much water for her and for me, for both of us, she said, we ought to share it.

How, I asked, did she imagine that might happen?

Oh, it was simple. At last she knew how she could thank me: by repaying me in kind. She actually used that phrase. She had nothing else to offer, she said. Imagine, she suggested spontaneously; no, she decided, how can I put it, she made up her mind to wait for me beside the lake. If she were to die before me, as she was convinced she would. Then I could still decide whether to swim across the lake with her to Paradise or wait for my husband in spite of everything, but then I'd be sure to go to Hell with him.

In fact, Schepp, she made the same pact with me as you once did. With the difference that she has no doubts about reaching the far shore. How firmly she pressed my hand! More firmly than you, that's for sure.

So let's be clear: when, one day, you set out on the journey to the next world, I will not be waiting for you at the threshold. Ditto the other way round. No need for you to wait for me. You have silently terminated our marriage in the Here and Now, I free you from your promise for There and Then. As far as I am concerned, and Dana is right there, you can go to –

No, even now I don't wish you that, I will concentrate entirely on what the signs, each in its own way, have shown me. The clock on the Church of the Good Shepherd is just striking eight-thirty, and my taxi will be coming in an hour's time, so I must hurry. My heart is thudding with anticipation, can you imagine that? Over the past year I've consulted the coins of the I Ching almost daily and have received all sixty-four signs as an answer to my only question. Each sign contributed to my decision. Think of the Wanderer, or the

Breakthrough, or Liberation. 'When there is nowhere left to go, then returning will save you. If there is somewhere you must go, then speed will save you.' How inspiring the signs can be. I never thought so before.

Yesterday evening I consulted the I Ching one last time, and – no, it did not give me the twenty-ninth sign as my answer; that would have been too much of a coincidence. It gave me Number 61, Inner Truth, a happy, cheerful water sign. As if everything from which I have suffered all my life will now be turned into its opposite, the gentle wind above, the rejoicing lake below. 'It is good to cross the great water.' But without you, Schepp, do you understand, without you. As far as I'm concerned, and now I will say it once and for all, you can go straight to Hell! Along with

Hanni and Nanni and Lina and Tina and
whatever they might be called. Your
I'm sorry, my head
suddenly hurts again
like when I

Yes, Doro had actually written that. The spaces between the words had become longer and longer, and at the bottom of the page they were in an entirely different handwriting. Schepp had already deciphered them:

and now this too
well we'll
talk about it

There was no more to be deciphered, to be read. Schepp just sat there. While the afternoon cast its shadows little by little over the pattern of the parquet, while the clock of the Church of the Good Shepherd struck four high and five low notes, while there was another ring of the doorbell, while the last large patches of light merged under the desk, while there was a buzzing and then silence, then buzzing again and then more silence. She had him now.

How peacefully she lay there, how detached, as if none of it had anything more to do with her. Yet she had caused it. Unmoved herself, she had been the guiding spirit, so surely it was her fault? Her eyes, mere slits like a lizard's eyes now, the whites slyly showing, her nose, sharper still in the twilight; her head a skull carved out of the room's half-light. Doro? Schepp stared at her, although he had no idea what he might still be looking for in her face. All that he had seen in it unquestioningly over the years, over the decades, had perhaps been a show staged just for him. All he could really do was stare into space until darkness fell.

Stop, Schepp! At least it was over and done with, he had performed his final duty. Now he knew that Doro had had no premonition of her death, that instead she had been editing and writing her way towards a new life. He knew why the doorbell had rung earlier, and what kind of post he might expect to receive soon. Schepp closed his eyes, imagined Dana kissing Doro, raising one leg as she did so and ... then he imagined Doro kissing Dana. Although she had made it clear that the whole thing had been platonic. In so far as he had understood it correctly. In so far as she had not been lying. In so far as she had not just wanted to spare him. Schepp pictured Doro lying on that very same *chaise-longue*, thinking of Dana, thinking of kissing her, which was almost as bad.

When he opened his eyes again – only because he felt a cold draught streaming towards him – he found himself kneeling on the floor, his head buried in the hollow at the base of Doro's throat, his arm firmly around her rigid shoulders. He immediately relaxed this ardent embrace and looked at Doro sternly, questioningly, imploringly, but her waxen face did not respond. Then he sought certainty by sniffing frantically as if that would help him discover what she had taken with her as her secret. There was still a familiar scent about her although the penetratingly bad smell that didn't blend comfortably with it was getting stronger, mingling with the traces of her perfume, a sweetish drift of that aroma. Schepp inhaled it like a man newly in love, stopped abruptly, looked at Doro, whispered to her: You are right, when you can't smell other people, you're really dead, how sad.

She was rigid all over now, completely cold. When he checked one last time to see whether her hands were still folded, or rather lying hooked together, large marks of *livor mortis* had emerged over her entire body. The discolouration had made rapid progress. All at once he shivered; he went to the window to close it, then abruptly opened it again.

Yes, that was better. Standing at the window and looking down into the street, Schepp realized that he was now much worse off than he had been in the morning. He had been deserted twice over, a man who had even lost his wife. His wife, what an unthinkable thought! She had fallen hook, line and sinker for Dana and her fairy tales, today she had come close to setting out in pursuit of a chimera. Should he be relieved that Death had intervened, sparing him that humiliation at least?

Standing at the window looking down into the street, Schepp realized that things were even worse than that. For he had also lost Dana again today, more finally than the first time. Jealousy was added to disgrace. She might not have, well, indecently assaulted his wife, but what of it? She had revenged herself thoroughly; her lying tales of his 'affairs and would-be affairs' had played a considerable part in what had happened to Doro. To Doro and to him. Or in what had not happened. How could Dana have hated him so much, when apart from a silly misunderstanding – and a slap in the face, admittedly – there had been nothing at all between them? Well, almost nothing.

There he stood, the betrayer betrayed and at odds with himself. Hadn't Doro's betrayal been much more complete than his? Wasn't life nothing but betrayal? And, even more, being betrayed? And hadn't he known it all along? Known that even behind Doro's everyday smile some kind of abyss lay waiting. In the end, of course, she too had been taken in by Dana's lies and, above all, had been abandoned. There Schepp stood at odds with himself. Yet for all the thoughts of Doro and Dana that flashed through his mind, he could no longer deny what had happened. He had lost them both twice over – Dana a few years before, but really only now, Doro a few hours before, but really only now.

'High time,' he heard himself suddenly announcing to the chestnut trees, 'high time I get her out of my sight.' He turned back, took a step towards the desk, he'd get the doctor, and if the undertaker wanted to come too, fine with him. Doro's remains had to go right away. Right away.

Out of the way.

Or should he first correct her corrections to *Marek the Drunkard*? Then tear up each page into tiny scraps? How difficult it was to gather all the pages of the manuscript again, not at all easy to pretend you were just picking up some scattered bits of paper. When had he dropped them? Why were they thrown all over the room? So many sheets of paper. So many.

Eventually it become easier, faster. Schepp glided across the parquet, was almost hovering in the air, swirling and fluttering and prancing, pirouetting around all the little dishes and shells and candle-holders and copper plates that he had collected for years, and that were now arranged anew on the floor. He apologized to each item with a polite little bow, welcomed every sheet of paper with open arms, picking it up, reading its number out loud. In the end he was holding the complete manuscript again. Or at least what he thought was the manuscript.

At least now I know why I wrote it, he told himself wrathfully. Because with Hanni and Nanni and Lina and Tina and whatever they might be called – how did it go on? No, I wanted to have something I could roll up at the right moment. And with this rolled-up manuscript he struck himself, his leg, his arm, his stomach, his forehead, keeping time with his bafflement. And felt nothing. He saw the fly settling nearby, his gesticulations didn't shoo it away, so he killed it. More as part of the time he was beating than as a deliberate act, a matter of course; he didn't really notice that he'd done it.

Before he could go completely mad he sat down on the floor, leaned against one of the shelves at the far end of the room, as far from the *chaise-longue* as possible, surrounded by the scattered testimony to his life. Hadn't he wanted to say a dignified goodbye? Bitterness overwhelmed him, bitterness at having missed out on the most important thing, something that could no longer be questioned, no longer be rectified. Being dead, he thought, means first and foremost that you can't apologize, can't forgive and be reconciled, there's nothing left to be forgiven, only to be forgotten. Or rather there's nothing to be forgotten, only forgiven. None the less, he suddenly heard himself quietly asking Doro to forgive him, assuring her of his love, thanking her for having been there, for staying with him for so long.

After that he was so tired. Marvelled at the gentle mood of the late afternoon, the mild light, the fresh air trying to mingle with the musty process of decomposition that had quietly set in. How easy everything was suddenly, because it was so difficult, wasn't that so? Schepp was talking to himself, Schepp was beside himself. In the golden glow of glorious autumn, the first shadows were getting ready to emerge from the corners of the room and then to gather quickly. The street lights would be on soon outside, a damp mist would settle on the streets and fog creep out of front gardens. Did he want to pray? Yes, very much, but to what god? Schepp was alone in the world, entirely alone, inconsolably alone, powerless. He had to accept how even inanimate objects recoiled from him, the walls, even what was closest to him, seemed immeasurably far away, to be reached only by dint of great effort and self-abnegation. There was nothing to do but sit here in reverence and wait until the pattern of the parquet had dispersed entirely in the twilight. Then maybe he would be able to fly, or to fall. If on the balance sheet of life everything sooner or later had to be paid for, had an invisible price to be paid sooner or later, if every hour of happiness had to be weighed up against ten of unhappiness – then for twenty-nine years he had been happy (or maybe a few years less, never mind, came to the same thing), so he might as well be unhappy for the rest of his life, it was only fair.

Then he didn't think any longer, he only sat. Sat and gazed into the eternal process of birth and decay or whatever it was all fundamentally about, linking one thing with another, that one with yet another, flowing over and into it, mingling and dispersing and in the end leaving only a continuous grey expanse. It was quiet inside him now, there wasn't a breath of air. He was no longer searching its darkest folds and the gloom could rise and spread. Soon he was filled with darkness, held frozen until the day when he, too, would –

Before he withdrew into this darkness, it occurred to Schepp that he could hope for nothing on this day, that he was abandoned even for the time after death, and once there he would have an eternity in which to settle his accounts, in the next world too he would have to pay with unhappiness for the happiness he had accepted unthinkingly in this life, in the end had gambled away. He almost ventured a little laugh, almost. But in fact he observed total silence as he waited for night to fall, and as the silence rose around him he thought again of Doro's cold, dark lake. Thought of himself standing on its shore, thought how he would have to enter it alone, and suddenly he began to shiver. How clammy he felt; was this possible? Then he started, opened his mouth wide and gasped.

The lake lay before him.

The lake about which he had heard so much, about which he had thought and spoken so often, the lake in which, all the same, he had never entirely believed. For the first time he no longer had to imagine what it might look like, he *saw* it, the lake was there. How vast it was! How beautiful! The pull it exerted was powerful, unmistakable, it was drawing him towards it. Schepp scrambled up, Schepp got to his feet. But wasn't he mortally afraid? He would have preferred to stay where he was, dissolving into the landscape that he guessed was there as a backdrop to the lake. In fact he couldn't see anything. No bleak, rocky mountain panorama, no shadowy outlines of mountain pines, least of all an island or a far shore. Only the lake's frosty desolation. Above it a wan sky without moon or stars, distant lightning flashing through it as if a great brightness were breaking beyond the horizon, its reflection lighting the scene. A rustling somewhere, something crackling in the undergrowth or an owl hooting, that wouldn't have surprised him, but all he could hear was that there was nothing to be heard, nothing at all. A deathly silence. How unruffled was the lake's glittering surface! A leaden silver covered it, and beneath it waited the death that came after death. Schepp's skin prickled even though he hadn't yet taken off his clothes. If Doro's little hand had been within reach, he would have taken it and held it as tightly as he possibly could have done. The lake was far too dark for one soul alone, and cold. He knew merely by looking at it that it was cold.

If only it hadn't been for that smell! As if Doro had forgotten to change the water for the flowers, as if their stems had begun to rot overnight, filling the air with the sweet-sour aroma of decay. Schepp noticed it at once, that subtle sense of something Other in the midst of ordinary life, slightly skewing the morning. The darkness of his dreams had affected him powerfully, he had awakened in fear several times, had just now nearly fallen out of bed as a result. He had forgotten to put on his glasses, but he had no problem finding the way; after all it had been his way into the new day for almost thirty years and he knew every segment in the parquet by its creaking. Autumn brightness shone from the far end of the room, turning every object into some sparkling, blurry entity, eventually merging into diffuse patches of colour, and the urgency of the world was muted for Schepp to a few brown, beige and gentle golden hues. On the other hand, nearly blind as he was, he could distinguish the specific aromas of the old books, the furniture, the *chaise-longue* all the more distinctly. He immediately picked up Doro's scent, even though he couldn't see her anywhere he knew that she was there, probably sitting at his desk. Schepp stopped, squinting so that he could at least discern outlines, and as he checked the way his hair lay over his bald patch, stroking the back of his head, he told himself that this morning he was a happy man.

Not least because of Doro, whose own pinned-up hair, mingled black and silver, he could see above the back of the desk chair. At one side he glimpsed the kimono she liked to wear when she sat in that chair, editing what he had written the day before. Obviously she had dropped off to sleep; he wondered what she had found to edit on their return from yesterday's visit to the doctor; he had not gone back to his desk himself.

Schepp continued his careful walk across the fishbone pattern of the parquet, always expecting to collide with something or stumble over some object that happened to be in his way. Although he could only vaguely make out the sun, the desk, the vase standing on the floor with the rotting gladioli in it, the chair with Doro's shock of hair, it suddenly all seemed as familiar to him as if he had already seen it once before in exactly the same way, smelt it the same way, experienced it in the same sequence.

Before he planted a kiss on her neck, stealing up quietly like a man newly in love, a fly buzzing somewhere (but even that sounded oddly, bizarrely, familiar), before he bent over Doro, to the little mole at the base of her throat that he knew so well – any minute now she would wake with a start and look askance at him, half indignant, half affectionate – he suddenly registered a stack of paper on the desk, recognizable as a vaguely rectangular pale shape. He was about to pick it up when, quite suddenly, yesterday's visit to the new ophthalmologist in the old familiar practice came into his mind, and the advice he had so emphatically given. Schepp remained behind the chair where Doro was sitting so still. Yes, Hinrich, he grinned in the direction where he guessed the shape of a great future might be, at the age of sixty-five you're not too old to start a new life, what a prospect. He finally leaned over Doro. Once again the smell hit him, almost overpowering in its piercing sweetness, as if … as if he had smelt it before. Schepp shrank back.

'What's that stink – er, what's that you're editing?'

'Just what I'm wondering myself,' replied Doro as quickly as if she had been pretending to be asleep, had just been waiting for this moment. She didn't look up, but gathered the manuscript and held it close to his face. 'You never told me about this! Did you ever write any more such – such – '

Schepp was quick to say no, he had not, and this dated from a long time ago, he had forgotten all about it.

What, she asked, about the woman in it?

Dana? Schepp vaguely surmised; was he still dreaming? Or dreaming again? 'Yes, of course, her most of all, oh yes.' To think that Doro wanted to walk into the lake with her! 'As if someone like that would accompany you more surely to the far shore – Dana of all people!'

'Dana? Who's she?' Doro cocked her head, most likely regarding him sternly. 'I thought her name was Hanni!' As for the lake, she and he were going there together, they'd agreed that ages ago, surely he hadn't forgotten?

How cool her voice sounded! Schepp knew just what she looked like at this moment; she was almost certainly gazing at him fixedly, gently, firmly. The clock of the Church of the Good Shepherd struck four high notes and eleven low ones, he counted them automatically, and the fly went on buzzing. Doro stood up and came so close to him that he could make out the expression on her face.

'Hinrich, you haven't got your glasses on, you can't even see me.'

She meant it seriously, no question of that. Schepp knew her tone, her look, her way of tracing a little curve through the air with her hand.

'And how did you know I was reading one of your manuscripts? What's more, how did you know which one?'

Schepp tried to think. No answer came to him; something was not quite right this morning. Perhaps it had to do with that smell. 'Listen, Doro, can't you smell it? I mean, there's a stink as if something had died and was lying under the sofa.'

'Hinrich, that's not something you ought to say, not something you even ought to think!' Then, with an ostentatious sniff, Doro inhaled and nodded. Yes, she said, she could smell it too, how strange. As if she'd forgotten to change the water in the flower vase and during the night the stems ...

Schepp put his hand to his head, could only feel a few strands of hair. Somehow or other he couldn't seem to get the hang of today, that remark seemed familiar as well, had Doro said it to him once before?

'But I *didn't* forget,' she said, justifying herself more for her own sake than for his. 'It can't be the gladioli.'

What, then? She seemed to become angry, took a few steps backwards and then forwards, came back, kimono wrapped tightly around her as if she were freezing, scanned the room looking for some object that could be blamed for the smell. Not finding anything, she became even more agitated. Schepp couldn't see it, he felt it from the tone in which she spoke to herself, so cool, so unyielding, so impatient.

'Don't get angry, Doro,' he said, feeling clumsily for where he thought her hand might be. 'The doctor told you not to, and it's only – '

Now she was standing in front of him again, her kimono so blue, her skin shimmering almost white in the silky reflection, she must look wonderful. All at once he was terribly afraid for her. 'Think of your headaches, oh do.'

'Why do *you* want to know about my headaches all of a sudden?' Doro came so close to him that he couldn't help seeing her features. Her gaze rested inquiringly on him; she shook her head. 'Hinrich, do you by any chance have something to tell me?'

Before Schepp could answer, a slow smile spread across her face, beginning in the corners of her mouth, then growing up to the little lines at the corners of her eyes. Who knew why; Schepp never knew what to make of Doro's mood swings. Had he said something stupid? Done something funny? Never mind, the next moment she was smiling radiantly in her incomparable way, and he knew at once, and yet again, why he had fallen in love with her thirty years before and why he still loved her, he knew at once, to the tips of his toes, how good life was. The sun lay on the parquet and made it shine. Schepp closed his eyes. He would have to open a window to let all that happiness out again later.

Subscribe

Subscribe to Peirene's series of books and receive three world-class contemporary European novellas throughout the year, delivered directly to your doorstep. You will also benefit from a 40% members' discount and priority booking for two people on all Peirene events.

PEIRENE'S GIFT SUBSCRIPTION
Surprise a loved one with a gift subscription. Their first book will arrive tied with a beautiful Peirene ribbon and a card with your greetings.

The perfect way for book lovers to collect all the Peirene titles.

> 'What a pleasure to receive my surprise parcel from Peirene every four months. I trust Meike to have sourced for me the most original and interesting European literature that might otherwise have escaped my attention. I love the format and look forward to having a large collection of these beautiful books. A real treat!' GERALDINE D'AMICO, DIRECTOR, JEWISH BOOK WEEK

Annual Subscription Rates
(3 books, free p&p, 40% discount on Peirene events for two people)
UK £25   EUROPE £31   REST OF WORLD £34

Peirene Press, 17 Cheverton Road, London N19 3BB
T 020 7686 1941
E subscriptions@peirenepress.com

www.peirenepress.com/shop
with secure online ordering facility

Peirene's Series

FEMALE VOICE: INNER REALITIES

NO 1
Beside the Sea by Véronique Olmi
Translated from the French by Adriana Hunter
'It should be read.' GUARDIAN

NO 2
Stone in a Landslide by Maria Barbal
Translated from the Catalan by Laura McGlaughlin and Paul Mitchell
'Understated power.' FINANCIAL TIMES

NO 3
Portrait of the Mother as a Young Woman
by Friedrich Christian Delius
Translated from the German by Jamie Bulloch
'A small masterpiece.' TLS

....
MALE DILEMMA: QUESTS FOR INTIMACY

NO 4
Next World Novella by Matthias Politycki
Translated from the German by Anthea Bell
'Inventive and deeply affecting.' INDEPENDENT

NO 5
Tomorrow Pamplona by Jan van Mersbergen
Translated from the Dutch by Laura Watkinson
'An impressive work.' DAILY MAIL

NO 6
Maybe This Time by Alois Hotschnig
Translated from the Austrian German by Tess Lewis
'Weird, creepy and ambiguous.' GUARDIAN

SMALL EPIC: UNRAVELLING SECRETS

NO 7
The Brothers by Asko Sahlberg
Translated from the Finnish by Emily Jeremiah and Fleur Jeremiah
'Intensely visual.' INDEPENDENT ON SUNDAY

NO 8
The Murder of Halland by Pia Juul
Translated from the Danish by Martin Aitken
'A brilliantly drawn character.' TLS

NO 9
Sea of Ink by Richard Weihe
Translated from the Swiss German by Jamie Bulloch
'Delicate and moving.' INDEPENDENT

....
NEW IN 2013
TURNING POINT:
REVOLUTIONARY MOMENTS

NO 10
The Mussel Feast by Birgit Vanderbeke
Translated from the German by Jamie Bulloch
'Chilling precision.' DER SPIEGEL

NO 11
Mr Darwin's Gardener by Kristina Carlson
Translated from the Finnish by Emily Jeremiah and Fleur Jeremiah
'Effortless humour.' SUOMEN KUVALEHTI

NO 12
Chasing the King of Hearts by Hanna Krall
Translated from the Polish by Philip Boehm
'An outstanding writer.' GAZETA WYBORCZA

Peirene

Contemporary European Literature. Thought provoking, well designed, short.

'*Two-hour books to be devoured in a single sitting: literary cinema for those fatigued by film.*' TLS

Online Bookshop

Subscriptions

Literary Salons

Reading Guides

Publisher's Blog

www.peirenepress.com

Follow us on twitter and Facebook @PeirenePress
Peirene Press is building a community of passionate readers.
We love to hear your comments and ideas.
Please email the publisher at: meike.ziervogel@peirenepress.com